"I thin have an affair."

David spoke matter-of-factly. "Nothing earthshaking," he went on. "Just get each other out of our systems. Once the ritual's finished, of course."

Piper whirled to stare at him in astonished furor. "*What?* Are you insane?" she asked, shaking her head in dazed wonder. "First you insult me. You tear me practically to shreds. Now you ask me to have an affair?"

"I find you—attractive," he said, seizing her by the arm to keep her from leaving. "Whether or not we like it, there's something between us. Physically, that is. But I have to tell you up front that you're not the type I'd settle down with. Not the sort I'd marry."

Piper tossed him a brief, fiery glance. "Why would I want to have an affair with you? I'd rather have an affair with—with the devil."

When she tried to pull away, David drew her closer, his hands clamping over her upper arms. "Because you need to," he answered. "Because you want to."

Bethany Campbell, an English major and textbook consultant calls her writing world her "hidey-hole," that marvelous place where true love always wins out. Her hobbies include writing poetry and thinking about that little scar on Harrison Ford's chin. She laughingly admits that her husband, who produces videos and writes comedy, approves of the first one only.

Readers unanimously approved of Aaron Whitewater, Bethany's attractive hero in *The Lost Moon Flower*. And now you can meet Aaron's brother, David, in *The Cloud Holders*. We think you'll agree there's something special about the Whitewater men!

Books by Bethany Campbell

HARLEQUIN ROMANCE
2949—THE DIAMOND TRAP
3000—THE LOST MOON FLOWER
3019—THE SNOW GARDEN
3045—THE HEART OF THE SUN
3062—DANCING SKY
3079—THE ENDS OF THE EARTH
3109—EVERY WOMAN'S DREAM

HARLEQUIN INTRIGUE
65—PROS AND CONS
116—THE ROSE OF CONSTANT
151—DEAD OPPOSITES

THE CLOUD HOLDERS
Bethany Campbell

Harlequin Books

TORONTO • NEW YORK • LONDON
AMSTERDAM • PARIS • SYDNEY • HAMBURG
STOCKHOLM • ATHENS • TOKYO • MILAN

ISBN 0-373-03133-5

Harlequin Romance first edition July 1991

THE CLOUD HOLDERS

CHAPTER ONE

VALUES! VALUES! VALUES! cried the sign in the jewelry-store window. Beneath it sparkled a rich display of diamonds and sapphires, platinum and gold.

Piper Gordon didn't like the sign. To her, it lacked dignity, lacked finesse. But her grandmother had insisted that the sign was an excellent idea, so Piper didn't object. Someday she would be in charge and things would be done her way. Until then, she would shrug off all minor misgivings.

Disagreeing with Eloise Claxton took enormous energy, so Piper bothered to do so only over matters of great importance. When the occasion demanded, she could be as stubborn, strong and dauntless as the woman who had raised her. It was no mean feat.

Now, sitting on one of the Jacobean chairs in her grandmother's office one Friday afternoon in March, she knew the two of them must clash. There was no helping it.

"No," Piper said with determination. "Absolutely not."

"Yes," said Eloise with even greater determination. The air shimmered with tension.

Piper's hands clenched the chair's scrolled arms. "No," she repeated, shaking her head for emphasis.

She was a woman of twenty-four, slender and of average height. She looked somewhat out of place in the office, for she was the only thing in it with smooth clean lines.

Her silky brown hair was cut nearly as short as a boy's and fell across her forehead in neat bangs. Her regular features were beautiful rather than pretty; she had excellent bone structure and flawless skin. Everything about her looked trim, tidy and well-controlled. Everything, that is, except her blue eyes, which flashed with rebellion.

Piper lifted her chin at a defiant angle. "You can't give away something worth fifty thousand dollars. You expect me to run things someday. I can't stand by and let you *do* this."

Eloise eyed her granddaughter balefully. She was shorter than Piper, heavier and more sharply featured. Her snow white hair was elaborately curled. Diamonds, a good many of them, glittered on her fingers and ears and throat. She sat with one foot propped on a velvet stool.

"You're not in charge of things yet," Eloise said, narrowing her eyes. "I am. And I have *no* choice in this."

"I've never known you not to have a choice." Piper's tone was sardonic, almost light, but in truth she was worried. Her grandmother was usually full of fight, but lately she seemed tired, distracted and unpredictable. Piper, who loved her, hated seeing her so unlike herself.

"It's the law." Eloise leaned back in her ornately carved chair in disgust.

Piper could sit still no longer. She rose and paced the office. Eloise collected things, and Piper sometimes felt trapped and smothered by the number of objects in the room. Her own office, down the hall, was as neat and uncluttered as Piper herself.

She stopped beside an antique filing cabinet and picked up a porcelain figurine of a frog bowing to a queen. "Laws can be changed," she said. "They can be challenged. You've done it before."

"Not this time," Eloise said fretfully. "Nobody's challenged it successfully so far. Why should I try? It'd cost me more than the thing is worth. Put down that figurine, Piper. You'll break it."

Piper placed the figurine beside a silver snuffbox. "What are museums going to do?" she demanded, trying to spark her grandmother's old fire. "Give away millions of dollars worth of artifacts? What about the Smithsonian? They have a huge Indian collection."

"That's the Smithsonian's problem, not mine," Eloise said, and winced when she tried to shift positions. She had gout, and recently it had flared up badly. Her bare foot, propped on the stool, was swollen, and lately the only way she could walk was by hobbling about with a cane.

"Ouch," Eloise grimaced, then swore under her breath. "My only problem—other than my own toe's trying to assassinate me—is getting rid of one ugly necklace." She winced again. "The natives," she said between her teeth, "are restless."

Piper sighed in frustration.

Nebraska had recently passed a law requiring the return of Native American remains and grave goods to their rightful tribes. Skeletons and burial objects were being stripped from museums and private collections, and sent back for proper disposal.

Piper shook her head again. She folded her arms and stepped to the wall where a plain black shadow-box frame hung amid a cluster of more ornately framed objects.

Within the frame was a necklace. It was, as Eloise claimed, a rather ugly necklace. A crude silver chain linked irregular white pearls to imperfect black ones, uncut olivines of dull green, and polished twigs of black coral.

Piper didn't know a great deal about the necklace, only that it had always intrigued her and that it had something to do with a Hawaiian volcano goddess.

In all of Eloise's collection of overwrought Victorian knickknacks, paintings and antique jewelry, nothing had ever fascinated Piper as much as this old necklace. Among all the fringed lamp shades, filigreed music boxes and painted china figurines, it had stood out by reason of its primitive and powerful simplicity.

During her childhood, Piper had made up fantastic stories about the necklace. She'd daydreamed of pirates and handsome Hawaiian warriors, tropical islands, war canoes, and a beautiful princess with orchids in her hair.

The truth about the piece was less romantic than her fantasies, but still mysterious. The necklace had been created in the early nineteenth century as a gift for a Hawaiian chief. Its maker was a Portuguese sailor who had jumped ship in the Hawaiian islands, where he had earned a reputation as a local sorcerer.

The necklace was to have been disposed of in a ritual following the chief's death, but his grieving granddaughter had kept it hidden, in an effort to keep his spirit close to her.

What had happened to the necklace after she stole it, where it had vanished during the next century, nobody knew. It reappeared shortly after World War II, turning up unexpectedly in the possession of a woman named Maureen McMurphy Shimodo, a pearl dealer in Hawaii. Then, in the late 1960s, the dealer had the misfortune to fall in debt to Eloise Claxton, and the necklace became Eloise's.

Jewelry was both Eloise's business and her passion, and this piece, she said, was remarkable for one reason only: its rarity. Hawaiians had usually adorned themselves with flowers and feathers. This necklace, with its pearls from Tahiti, its extraordinary pieces of Hawaiian olivine and its complex connection to legend, was irreplaceable.

Piper studied the necklace and gritted her teeth. The piece was the only one of its kind, and Eloise had acquired it fairly. Now law demanded she give it up. What bothered Piper most was not that her grandmother must lose the necklace; no, there was something far more galling.

To fulfill its ritualistic purpose, the necklace had to be destroyed. The thought made Piper almost ill.

"It's not a law about art," she said, taking a deep breath to steady herself. "It's about graves. It's to keep those farmers who plow up Indian bones from sticking them in a barn and selling tickets to tourists. It has nothing to do with Hawaii."

Eloise frowned and rearranged her pleated skirt over her extended leg. "Hawaiians are Native Americans, too. That fool thing—" she made an impatient gesture toward the necklace "—is what lawyers called 'grave goods.' Now, all of a sudden, it's supposed to be disposed of. I don't like it any better than you do."

"It's criminal," Piper said, still staring unhappily at the necklace. Its gems were not strung, but crudely set in silver. The Portuguese sailor, so the legend went, had been some sort of smith's apprentice before he'd run off to sea.

"It's a criminal shameful *waste*," Piper went on, resentment smoldering. "This thing is historic. It should be left to a museum like the rest of your collection—it's one thing to give it to the Hawaiians—it's another thing to destroy it. That's . . . unspeakable."

"The museum will be getting quite enough when I die," Eloise replied with a flash of her old feistiness. "It'll have to make do with one less trinket. It's not important enough to fight over. Now if those Hawaiians wanted my diamonds, they'd have a battle on their hands. I'd teach them a thing or two about war chants."

Eloise had long intended for the family name to live on after she was gone. She had arranged to leave her money to the art museum; a new wing was to be built to house all the treasures of her private collection. It was her life's ambition and the consolation of her old age.

"I don't approve of this," Piper grumbled. She loved the necklace and wanted her grandmother to keep it, even if it meant a legal battle.

There was an ominous moment of silence.

"You may not approve of it," Eloise said carefully, stretching her arthritic fingers so that her diamonds sparkled, "but I want you to go to the islands. I want *you* to do it. Destroy it."

Piper stood up, aghast, staring at her grandmother's implacable face. A terrible uneasiness began to creep through her. "Me? *Me?*"

"You." Eloise nodded so that the light glinted on her sculpted curls. "These things are supposed to be done just so. When Maureen Shimodo turned the necklace over to me, she gave me papers outlining the whole sacrifice rigmarole—it's all documented—the Portuguese sailor wrote it down all those years ago. The Hawaiian Cultural Bureau verified it. Sit down and stop gaping at me, Piper. I dislike being gaped at."

"I'm not going anywhere," Piper protested, but she moved back to sit in the chair as if in a daze. "I'm supposed to be helping you run this jewelry store. I have... responsibilities."

"The store can spare you for a week." Eloise picked up a leather folder from her desk. Piper noted that her hands shook slightly with the effort. "I've had photocopies of all the documentation made for you, so that you'll get it exactly right. You leave on Monday. That gives you the weekend to get ready for the trip and to get Jeannie used to the idea."

Piper gripped the chair arms again, more tightly than before. "Jeannie?" she said, thinking of her aunt. "That's another reason I can't go. How will you deal with Jeannie? She's been impossible lately."

Piper's Aunt Jeannie had lived with Eloise and Piper for as long as Piper could remember. Jeannie had always been difficult, but recently she and Eloise had been getting on each other's nerves more than usual. It was up to Piper to preserve the shaky household peace.

"*I'll* keep an eye on Jeannie," Eloise said grimly. "It'll do her good not to be coddled for a change. Let's see, this is all quite ridiculous. It involves three islands. First you'll fly to Oahu. You have to talk to an old woman there who claims to be a volcano priestess. Then you have to drop the white pearls into the sea. Next it's on to the Big Island, Hawaii. You'll—"

"Drop the pearls into the sea?" Piper cried. "Take the necklace apart? Throw it away? That's insane. I can't do it—"

"I *want* you to do it," Eloise said with surprising harshness. "Then, on Hawaii you have to find a green sand beach and dispose of the black pearls."

"Green sand?" Piper said in disbelief. "There's no such thing as green sand."

"Piper, stop arguing. There *is* green sand on Hawaii—somewhere. You'll just have to find it. After Hawaii, you fly to Maui to dispose of the black coral. You must talk to another priestess. Then go up to the inactive volcano, break the black coral—"

"Break it?" Piper almost wailed.

Eloise set her jaw at a dangerous angle. Now that she had her dander up, she seemed almost her old invincible self. "Do you think *I* find this amusing? No. You smash the coral and fling it into the fool crater. Then it's back to Hawaii—"

"This is a wild-goose chase," Piper objected. "Throwing pearls into the ocean, smashing coral, talking to 'priestesses'—priestesses of what?"

"The volcano goddess," Eloise said irritably, "and no, don't tell me it's ridiculous to believe in a volcano goddess or a curse—I know it is. Nevertheless, once you return to the Big Island—"

"Curse? *Curse?*"

"Piper, stop fussing. Of course there's a curse or some such silliness. I told you—according to the beliefs of the time, certain rituals had to be followed to free the souls of the dead. The parts of the necklace are gifts to Pele, the volcano goddess, and she's said to be vengeful when she doesn't get what's hers. It's all superstition, and not very interesting superstition at that."

So that explains what's been wrong with this family all these years, Piper thought with dark sarcasm. Eloise offended the volcano goddess, and we've been in trouble ever since. How simple. How clear. Why didn't we realize it sooner?

"At any rate—" Eloise flinched as if the pain in her foot became particularly intense "—Oouf! At any rate," she went on, an edge in her voice, "then you go back to the Big Island, contact yet another priestess, and throw the olivine into the active volcano. Then you come home. It's done."

Piper sat poised in the chair, still gripping its arms. "Not the olivine," she insisted. "Those are extraordinary pieces of Hawaiian olivine. You hardly ever see pieces that large— you told me so yourself. No."

Eloise's eyes flashed with futile anger. "I hate losing the olivine. But it has to be done." The rebellious emotion in her face dimmed as rapidly as it had risen. She suddenly looked small and old.

"You shouldn't have to lose any of it," Piper said passionately. "You should go to court—"

"I told you," Eloise said with a tired wave of her hand, "if I fought, it'd cost me three times what the necklace is worth. No. I'm tired of fighting. You have to go. The ritual demands it."

Piper threw her hands up in dismay. "Ritual? What do we have to do with a ritual that some...some Portuguese deserter made up almost two hundred years ago? We have *work* to do. The spring sales are coming up. Jeannie has all those dental appointments, and you know she won't go alone. And something has to be done about the twins' glasses. I *can't* leave—"

Piper stopped, shocked to see the glimmer of moisture in her grandmother's eyes. Tears? she thought in disbelief— no, that was impossible. She had never seen Eloise cry. Never. She had only even heard of her crying once.

Sorrow warred with stubbornness on the older woman's face. "I can't help it," Eloise said, her voice sharp. "The ritual says a member of this family has to return the neck- lace—in person—as an act of penance. I have no choice but to depend on you."

Piper stared at her, numbed. *A family member,* she thought, her mind reeling. *A family member.*

Eloise read her look and understood it. "Yes," she said with acrimony. "I can't exactly call on any of my children, can I?"

Piper swallowed. Eloise had been successful in business, but her family had given her few rewards. Of her three off- spring, one was dead, one barely spoke to her, and the third was as dependent as a small child.

"Nor," Eloise said, her voice shaking, "can I exactly ask my other grandchildren to do it. Can I?"

Piper shifted in the chair uncomfortably. Eloise had three other grandchildren. Piper's older brother, Harold, was married, and he and his wife expected their first child within the month; he certainly couldn't leave at a time like this. Besides, although Piper loved Harold, she had to admit he was a bit of a harebrain. That was why Eloise had trained Piper to take over the business. Harold would probably never master anything more complicated than clerking in one of Eloise's smaller stores.

"Harold can't go," Eloise said rather acidly. "I wouldn't trust him to do it, anyway. He'd fall into a volcano. What other choice do I have?"

Piper bit the corner of her lip. She also had twin cousins, several years younger than she was. Donny and Ronny were Aunt Jeannie's children. But it was impossible for either Donny or Ronny to go. Severely retarded, they had been institutionalized for years. Ensuring they had the best of care was one of the many burdens Eloise had carried for years.

That left nobody to go to Hawaii. Except Piper. No, she thought in sick panic; her grandmother was asking her to do the unthinkable. "I can't destroy that necklace," she said, shaking her head. "I couldn't allow it. No. Let's fight this thing."

"I *won't* fight," Eloise said with such intensity that Piper flinched. "I've had enough of courts to last me a lifetime. There's only one solution. Somebody has to go to Hawaii. You."

Piper could only stare at her grandmother in disbelief. "No," she almost whispered, tears beginning to burn her own eyes. "I can't."

Eloise hurled her a glance of angry impatience. "Piper!"

Piper couldn't bring herself to answer. She had said the only thing she could say.

"Very well," Eloise said, her voice shaking with emotion. "If you won't, I'll do it myself."

"You *can't*," Piper objected, now torn in two directions. "It'd wear you out. You'd be in pain every inch of the way. That's imposs—"

"At my age," Eloise said with cold passion, "I'm not exactly a stranger to pain. Or having to depend on only myself." She tried to change positions in her chair, but even that slight movement caused her to wince.

Piper felt as if a stone had suddenly materialized in her throat. Her grandmother hadn't used this tone with her in years, not since Piper had insisted on going away to college. Piper had persisted until she'd won, then gone on her merry way to Chicago to study art history. But less than six months later, Eloise had become entangled in a legal and business setback. Eloise had been embroiled in legal squabbles before, but this one had been so traumatic it had nearly hospitalized her. Piper, alarmed, had rushed home, and she hadn't left her grandmother since.

Eloise sat up straighter, rebuke flashing in her eyes. "I've always counted on you to be the sensible one in this family," she said, her voice shaking with emotion. "And I've counted on you to be the sensible one when I'm gone. Now I don't know—what will become of everything if you can't be relied on?"

Piper's heart shriveled at the question. She had always thought her grandmother was a woman of iron, and she admired her strength. Eloise's husband had died young, leaving her with three small children and a debt-ridden jewelry store. She had raised the children and forged the ailing business into a success, then into a prosperous chain of stores. She had done it all alone.

When Piper's mother's marriage and health failed, it was Eloise who took in her invalid daughter and two small children. She raised Harold and Piper and for three years cared for their mother, Maisie. When Maisie died, she sat through the funeral, Harold and Piper on either side of her, refusing to cry because it might upset them. "We hold our heads up in this family," she had said. "We take what fate has to give, and we keep going on." Harold didn't understand and cried, anyway, but Piper, as always, tried hard to follow Eloise's example.

Aunt Jeannie, who lived with Eloise, was now almost a recluse. Jeannie had been happily married, and pregnant when she and her husband were in a boating accident. He had been killed and Jeannie seriously injured. The twin boys were born with such extensive brain damage that doctors said they would probably never recognize the members of their own family, not even Jeannie. Jeannie never really recovered from the trauma. Again it was Eloise who took charge, taking in Jeannie and providing for the twins, as well.

Piper had learned early to look to Eloise for discipline and order in her life. She had trailed Eloise like a little shadow, admired her tremendously, and at Eloise's knee she learned her first lessons about life. To survive, you must be hard-headed and strong. You run your business and family with an iron hand. You take care of your own, and you do whatever has to be done. You do it without complaint, without help from outsiders, and you don't show your emotions to the world.

"If only MacDowell were here," Eloise had often said in particularly trying times. But her son, MacDowell, was not there; he and Eloise had quarreled about money long ago, and he'd left Nebraska, vowing never to return. Eloise grieved because she had loved him best, and her daughters had grieved, as well. MacDowell had been the darling of the family, Eloise's great hope for comfort and support in the future.

With MacDowell gone, there had been nobody left in the family for Eloise to depend on; no one except Piper, who had still been a child. Harold was sweet, but vague and without ambition. Only Piper had shown signs that she was capable of growing up to fill the void left by MacDowell. And all of Piper's life, she had striven to be as much like Eloise as possible: fearless, self-sufficient and dependable.

Now, suddenly, on this dark and gloomy Friday afternoon, Eloise no longer seemed strong. She seemed resigned, unhappy and weary.

The stone that lodged in Piper's throat grew larger and harder. Eloise looked hopeless and resentful; perhaps she was far more tired and ill than Piper had suspected. The thought was frightening.

"I . . ." Piper began, then shook her head helplessly. She couldn't waste all that time and so much of her grandmother's money flying to Hawaii. Not just so she could senselessly destroy a work of art. She couldn't.

Eloise stared at her a long moment, her chin trembling. Suddenly the tears welled again in her eyes, and this time they threatened to spill over. "Don't say anything," she ordered. "Just go home. I want to be alone."

"I . . ." Piper was overwhelmed by guilt. How could she fail Eloise, who had given her everything?

"I . . ." she tried again, but the words choked in her throat. She couldn't destroy the necklace, not even for her grandmother. Could she?

Eloise stared off into the cluttered shadows as if she saw her long sad life somewhere in them. She sighed again, the sound of a strong woman who must relinquish more than she could bear. She took a deep breath. "Jeannie claims I've kept you tied too close to me. That someday you'd rebel. All right. Have your little rebellion over a foolish necklace. Have things your way. I won't beg you. I can do it myself." Again she shifted her position, and again she flinched with pain.

Piper felt battered, a bit sick. She knew, then, that she would go to Hawaii, whether she wanted to or not, that she would destroy the necklace whether she wanted to or not. She had to, to protect her grandmother; she hadn't seen Eloise this upset in years.

"I'll go, I'll go," Piper said, hating the tears that sparkled in her grandmother's proud eyes. "I didn't want to stay here because of myself. . . ."

Eloise dabbed the tears away with a linen handkerchief, obviously angry at the emotion she had shown. "*I'm* not giving the necklace away—or spending all this money to return it—for myself, either. I'm doing it because I have to."

Her voice almost broke on the last sentence. She raised her chin, her mouth set grimly. She didn't look at Piper. "Sometimes, when I'm alone and in pain, I think maybe that fool superstition is right. Maybe I have been cursed since I got that necklace. Heaven knows it never did Maureen Shimodo much good—the only way she could get out of debt was to give it up. The year I took possession of it was the year your mother got sick and your father left. Then Jeannie had her accident. And your Uncle MacDowell told me he'd never stay in Nebraska to run the business. So many troubles." She shook her head, her face taut with unhappy memories.

Piper rose and went to her grandmother's side. She put her hand on Eloise's shoulder and gave it a squeeze. "Don't say such things. Every family has its problems. I wasn't trying to be spiteful. I just hate to see the necklace destroyed. That's all."

Eloise shook her head. She still didn't look at Piper, but her voice softened. "I'm old. I'm tired. There are so many things to tend to. So many things. Now this. Sometimes it becomes almost too much. I've lost so much in my time. Well, what's one small necklace to me?"

She lapsed into silence again, brooding. Piper gave her shoulder another squeeze. "You can depend on me. You always have. I just...I just...it's all...it all seems so needless."

Piper threaded her way through the office's crowded furniture and walked again to the wall where the necklace hung. She stared at it, realizing now that it was largely responsible for Eloise's recent mood.

"I have more bad news," Eloise said, her voice harsher than before. "You won't be going alone."

Piper turned to stare at her grandmother in confusion. Her apprehension deepened. "What do you mean?"

"I mean," Eloise said, folding her handkerchief distractedly, "you have to be accompanied. In fact, originally you were supposed to be accompanied by two people."

"What?" Piper asked, a frown creasing her smooth brow.

"This is supposed to be supervised, from beginning to end, by a representative approved by the Hawaiian Cultural Bureau," Eloise said, her tone acrimonious. "You're also supposed to have a guardian from your own region. The Cultural Bureau's shown *some* mercy for an old woman, however. They'll accept a qualified Native American from this area to do both jobs—to represent the bureau and be the guardian."

"A Native American? An Indian?" Piper asked, disbelief overwhelming her uneasiness. "Just because some old fraud pretended to be a wizard, I'm flying to Hawaii with an Indian—and throwing away a fortune?" She made an impatient gesture. "Excuse me. Yesterday my life made sense. Today I'm trapped in a farce. So who's this...this chaperon?"

Eloise's face went bitter once more and her lips twisted in sarcasm. "A man whose integrity is *supposed* to be flawless. According to the bureau. He's to see that the ritual's carried out. That nobody cheats."

"I resent this," Piper said with spirit. "It's as if *I* can't be trusted. Who's this person?"

Eloise's face went stony and blank. She ran her hand over her silver curls. "He's a lawyer. He works with the Native American Legal Claims Organization. His name—" she paused and adjusted her skirt over her extended leg again "—his name is Whitewater. David Whitewater."

Piper felt a strange mingling of numbness and heightened sensation. Surely her grandmother hadn't uttered that particular name. Surely, she hadn't said that *David Whitewater* would accompany her to Hawaii. No, most certainly,

Piper would awaken at any moment, safe in her routine re-
alistic responsible world.

"Grandmother," she said with exaggerated calm, "I remember that name. You *hate* that man. He's the one who
took you to court over that Indian jewelry. He cost you a
small fortune. And he didn't do the business any good,
either. He nearly put you in the hospital."

Eloise raised her chin higher than before, and her mouth
curved down at the corners. "Yes. Well, I've seen his work
firsthand, haven't I? I was framed on that charge, Piper,
don't you ever forget it. I was victimized by that dealer from
Santa Fe, and then by Whitewater in the courtroom. How
did I know the silly stuff was made in Japan?"

"You couldn't have," Piper soothed. She knew how upset her grandmother became when she remembered the case
over the turquoise jewelry. Eloise had actually broken down
on the stand and wept in frustration and confusion. She had
been cheated and had meant to cheat no one, she said, but
for some reason her records concerning the jewelry had been
atypically sketchy. She had no way to prove her innocence.

David Whitewater had been merciless. And by being
merciless, he had won. Eloise had paid a heavy fine and
suffered a spate of damaging publicity. This was the case
that had made her grandmother so ill that Piper had come
back from Chicago and had never returned.

"I don't forgive him for what he did to me," Eloise said
with malice. "But *they* recommended him—I have no say in
it. But then, neither does he. He didn't want to go. But his
precious claims organization insists."

Her grandmother almost smiled. Piper didn't understand.

"So you needn't worry, Piper," Eloise said. "You'll be in
the hands of the absolutely 'incorruptible' Mr. Whitewater."

"I don't want to be in anybody's hands," Piper protested. "Especially his. You always talked as if he was an ogre. He's our *enemy*."

Her grandmother's ghostly smile faded and a look of rancor took its place. "Yes. Remember that. I happen to know he resents this errand as much as you do. He's a man of reason, not superstition. He'll feel far sillier than you doing all this—at least he should. And I have the small satisfaction of making him run around like a chicken with its head cut off. We'll see how he likes his precious Native American ritual when he has to carry it out himself."

Piper said nothing, only regarded her grandmother warily. Eloise's face was almost rigid with resentment.

"And," Eloise said, her eyes narrowing, "by giving him the fool thing, he won't have the pleasure of taking me to court again. I can deny him *that* much."

Suddenly Piper understood, and what she understood filled her with dismay. This was why Eloise wouldn't fight for the necklace in court. She was afraid to face David Whitewater again.

Piper was appalled. She had never known Eloise to fear anyone. This man had obviously bruised her grandmother's spirit more than she had realized.

"Is that why you won't challenge the law?" she asked softly. "You don't want to face him again?"

Eloise said nothing for a moment. Then she nodded, her expression more bitter than before. "Don't make this trip easy for him, Piper. He's proud and presumptuous, but you keep him in his place. You do that for me. Never forget who you are. And never forget what that man did to us."

Piper swallowed. "I won't," she promised.

"Good," Eloise said, and nodded. They sat in silence.

She's never been afraid of anything in her life, Piper thought, almost trembling with anger. Until now, when she's old and Whitewater comes along. I hate him.

Eloise's face softened slightly. "And if you could, some-how, save one little piece of the olivine for me. For a sou-venir. Just one. No one, surely, could begrudge me that much. Could they?"

"Of course not," Piper said mechanically, her mind still on the specter of the terrible David Whitewater. "You shouldn't have to forfeit any of it. It should all be yours by rights."

"Rights," Eloise said, weariness slipping back into her voice. "The word never seems to apply to me. Just save me one stone. That's all I ask."

Piper agreed. One piece of olivine. It seemed a small thing indeed for Eloise to ask. Piper would see that the wish was granted. She had to. She was expected to be the strong one now.

CHAPTER TWO

THE NOTE ARRIVED on Saturday. It was curt. "Meet me Monday morning at eleven o'clock in the lounge at the north end of the airport. Don't worry about finding me. I'll find you."

The dark blue handwriting coursed across the page, strong and spiky. The signature read "D. Whitewater." When the message had arrived, Piper felt it was high-handed and rude, so she refused even to think about the meeting. She thrust it out of her mind.

That had been Saturday. Now it was Monday, and her heart pummeled as she approached the more elaborate of the airport's two restaurants. She had already checked her luggage, and her left hand was locked around the handle of her carry-on bag. Her beige suede coat was draped over her right arm.

Her grandmother had been closemouthed about Whitewater. "You won't like him," was all she would say. "A nobody trying to be pushy. A rather ridiculous man, really, with all his causes, if he weren't so cruel. And then, of course, he *is* an Indian."

Eloise was of Scottish descent and in her veins ran some of the bluest blood of the British Empire. She was secretly snobbish to the marrow of her bones, although she was careful never to utter sentiments of prejudice outside the family circle. "This Whitewater's nothing but a glorified errand boy," Eloise kept saying. "Don't let him intimidate you. Remember who you are and you'll be fine. He may have worked against me before. This time I'm paying the bills, and he'll do as *I* say. Make him remember it. And don't let this trip be a pleasure for him.''

Piper had almost reached the lounge. Her footsteps seemed to echo ominously, but she knew she was being foolish. The airport hummed with activity; her footsteps sounded exactly the same as everyone else's.

Resentment of D. Whitewater festered within her. Last night he had come to Eloise's house and taken custody of the necklace; Piper was not to be trusted with it, a fact that had angered her. Eloise insisted the transaction be private. ''You'll get emotional,'' she told Piper. ''I know you. I have enough things to say to this Whitewater myself. I don't need your help.''

So now the necklace was gone, its journey toward destruction begun. And Whitewater, assigned to her like a guard to a prisoner, was to see that its destruction was complete. It made her almost sick with anger.

Nervousness about the flight churned within her, as well, and she realized uneasily that she didn't know what to expect of Whitewater. She imagined a portly middle-aged man, swarthy and humorless. She imagined him wearing an ill-fitting suit and a drab tie to show he was too idealistic to care about such fripperies as fashion. He would also wear too much turquoise jewelry to emphasize that he was Indian and proud of it.

Her eyes swept the lounge, which contained only a few people. None of them looked in the least like a humorless middle-aged Native American lawyer.

She stood uncomfortably in her beige suit and high heels, clutching the carry-on bag, too tense and irritated to know what to do. She supposed she should sit down and wait.

Suddenly she saw a movement at a table near the rear of the lounge. A dark-haired man raised his head and his blue eyes met hers and stayed locked with them for a long tingling moment.

Then he smiled.

No, Piper thought in confusion, he didn't really smile. But one corner of his wide mouth curved up almost imperceptibly, and a deep masculine dimple played in his right cheek.

When the blue eyes met hers, she'd felt their intensity so forcefully it was like a physical blow. Now his gaze flicked up, then down, her body. He nodded, a curt knowing motion.

Don't worry about finding me, he had written. *I'll find you.*

Piper knew that she'd been found.

She stood a little straighter in surprise. This man was neither middle-aged nor stolid-looking. He was tall and extremely broad of shoulder. He wore a dark blue sweatshirt with the silhouette of a howling wolf, an unzipped brown leather jacket, jeans and expensive running shoes. He sat, almost lounged, at the table, and he had been reading a paperback copy of *Gone with the Wind*. He wore no turquoise jewelry, only a watch.

A frisson of apprehension vibrated through her. Her grandmother had never mentioned that Whitewater was *young*. He couldn't be more than thirty-two or thirty-three. Nor had Eloise mentioned he was handsome, for Piper grudgingly had to admit that handsome he was.

The high cheekbones, the strong nose, the blue-black hair and slightly bronze cast of his skin marked him as part Indian. But the long-lashed electric-blue eyes, the slight wave to his thick hair, the dimple and the mocking set of his mouth indicated he was part white, as well.

When he stood, Piper was more disconcerted than before. He was tall, at least six foot three, and even from this distance she could tell he would tower over her. She ducked her head and made her way toward him, careful to keep her face blank.

Why hadn't Eloise mentioned how attractive the man was? Piper thought irritably. It distressed her to discover he was handsome, although she knew it shouldn't matter in the least. Eloise always said a man's looks were unimportant—unless he hoped to find a foolish rich girl and marry above himself. She said only two things about a man mattered—his bank balance and his power. Eloise was safely beyond the spell cast by mere looks.

Piper steeled herself to react the same way. Eloise always said to be suspicious of men; attentive ones were probably after the family money, and men in general, when one examined the family history, weren't dependable creatures. They were weak or they ran off or they died.

Piper reached Whitewater and raised her gaze to his. Once again she was shocked by the startling vibrant blue of his eyes.

"Piper Gordon?" he asked. His voice was low, with a slightly raspy resonating quality.

She nodded, keeping her chin high and her expression carefully composed. He seemed to appraise her coolness and find it unimpressive.

"David Whitewater," he said, and offered her his hand. She took it. It was a strong hand, lean, powerful and warm. Her own felt cold as death. When he released it, her fingers tingled as if tiny devils were pricking them with pitchforks.

"Have a seat," he said, pulling a chair out for her. She gave him a businesslike nod and sat primly, putting her bag on the floor beside her.

"Can I take that coat for you?" he asked with a politeness that sounded mechanical.

She shook her head. "I prefer to keep it," she said, rather grandly. She didn't want to accept favors from him, even small ones.

He settled into the chair across from her, crossing his arms over his broad chest. The look he gave her was long, studious and slightly cavalier. "Would you like a cup of coffee?"

The last thing Piper wanted was caffeine dancing through her nerves. She busied herself by smoothing out her coat in her lap. "No, thank you." Her voice was clipped.

He raised one dark brow. "I'm sorry we couldn't meet sooner. I had a lot of loose ends to tie up."

She tried to ignore his measuring stare. "You weren't too busy to pick up the necklace," she said, slipping the strap of her purse from her shoulder. She set it in her lap, where it perched awkwardly. She wished now she'd let him take her coat.

The black eyebrow arched a fraction of an inch higher. The corner of his mouth gave its almost imperceptible curl, and the dimple appeared, then vanished. "You don't sound any happier about it than your grandmother."

"Why should I?" Piper asked, disconcerted by his unwavering stare. "I'm a busy woman. I don't have the time to waste on superstitious...twaddle. Especially when it's costing my grandmother thousands of dollars. I can't believe she gave you the necklace."

He didn't bother to answer immediately. He signaled the waitress for more coffee and didn't speak until his cup was refilled.

"Your grandmother," he said out of the side of his mouth, "didn't give *me* anything. She's giving the necklace back to the Hawaiian people, to whom it belonged in the first place. And she's doing it because she knows it'd cost her more than it was worth to fight to keep it."

He shrugged as if that settled the matter.

"The difference between my grandmother and me," Piper informed him, "is that I wouldn't have given up. I'm not as tired as my grandmother. I'd have fought."

He shrugged again. The fugitive superior smile flirted with the corner of his mouth. "You might not be as tired, but you're not as smart, either. You'd lose."

Piper's nostrils flared. "So you'd like to think."

He set down his cup and gave her a sardonic look. "So I *know*. If you won in a lower court, I'd take you to a higher one. I'd drag you to the Supreme Court if I had to, where I'd beat your expensive little panties off."

She pressed her lips together in anger. "Sure of yourself, aren't you?" she said, her tone laced with false sweetness and real acid. "Just because you can bully an elderly woman, don't think you can bully me. I've heard how you treated her in court. It was shameless."

An expression of scorn passed over his face like a shadow. "What was shameless was the way she sniveled and sobbed and tried to play innocent. I didn't find her guilty, Miss Gordon. An impartial jury did. She said she was selling Navaho jewelry and that part of the proceeds went to Navaho schools. In truth she was selling jewelry made in Japan and all the profits went into her pocket."

"That's not true!" Piper said hotly. "She had no idea. Her supplier in Santa Fe had disappeared. He told her part of the price she paid went to charity. Then he went running off to Tokyo or someplace. He's the one who was guilty—"

He cut her off. "I already heard this again last night from your grandmother. She can't seem to let it go, either. But the case is over, Miss Gordon. Let's put it behind us. The necklace is another matter."

"It's another matter of taking something from my grandmother," Piper said bitterly.

"No." The wide mouth crooked scornfully. "It's a case of doing what's right. Can't you understand?"

"It's not right to take an old woman's valuable possession because of a bunch of hocus-pocus. I understand that much."

He looked away as if bored or disgusted. "Why do I sense the key word in that sentence was 'valuable'? Your family has a lot of money. Whatever this necklace is worth, it won't break you up in business. Or do you want to get *all* your grandmother's goodies when she's gone? Do you begrudge the Native Americans a scrap of their rightful religious heritage?"

Stung, Piper paled in anger. She stood to inherit little of her grandmother's money and none of her possessions; the museum would receive almost everything. That was what had caused the quarrel between Eloise and MacDowell so many years ago.

The family finances were none of Whitewater's business, and she refused to discuss them. She chose instead to attack him on the subject she instinctively knew would irritate him most. She remembered what Eloise had said about him being a rational, not a superstitious, man.

She straightened in her chair, her head tilted at an ironic angle. "Listen, I know you're very concerned about the Happy Hunting Ground—" she began, but he interrupted her with a suddenness that startled her.

"My beliefs aren't your concern, Miss Gordon. This is a matter of native rights. Get that straight." The edge in his voice was as dangerous as a razor, and it gave her pause.

"Listen," she said, her eyes narrowing exactly the way Eloise's did when angry, "you like to go on about 'rightful religious heritage.' Are you honest enough to admit what we're about to do is *silly?* Not merely wasteful, but downright stupid and *silly?*"

He flicked her a contemptuous glance. "Do you find everything you don't understand silly? This is a spiritual and cultural matter. But foremost, it's a legal one."

His coolness only increased her anger. "Noble words. I know that the Hawaiians used to practice human sacrifice. What if this so-called ritual said I had to be thrown into the ocean along with the pearls? Would you just say something exalted and toss me to the sharks?"

He set his jaw at a thoughtful angle. A deep line appeared between the dark brows. "A good question. They'd probably accept a reasonable substitute for you. Perhaps a nice little piglet." Idly he turned his attention across the room to something else.

Piper had been clutching her purse. Now she slammed it on the table, hard enough to make the coffee almost leap out of his cup.

"That was uncalled for!" she almost spat. "It was tasteless and *not* funny. It was also assinine and adolescent. Was it supposed to have some symbolic meaning? That my family are greedy capitalist pigs? Well, guess again, because most of my family are—"

He held up a hand to cut her off. His expression was one of strained patience. "I wasn't insulting you. You proposed an interesting legal problem. I offered a possible solution. An acceptable alternative sacrifice. Pork has always been a favorite sacrifice to the volcano goddess."

Piper shot him a rebellious look. "Well, I'm a rational informed person, and I don't believe in sacrificing anything—pig, person, or necklace. It's a silly belief and a sillier practice."

She thought anger flashed deep in his blue eyes and it gave her a prickle of illicit pleasure. He shifted his shoulders in a motion that told her he was keeping careful control of himself. But he smiled that one-cornered phantom of a smile she was quickly learning to hate.

"I'll bet you do silly things yourself, Miss Gordon."

"Don't bet," Piper said sweetly, tossing her bangs. "You'll lose your money."

David leaned his elbow on the table and rested his chin in his hand. Once more he studied her with disturbing thoroughness, his gemlike eyes cool and derisive.

"Let's see," he mused, his voice low. "For starters, I notice you've poked holes in your earlobes. Into those holes you've screwed objects of gold that seem to be shaped... Let me see, could those be four-leaf clovers in your ears, Miss Gordon? Is that silly? Or do you think they'll bring you luck?"

Piper glared at him. "You're talking about fashions, traditions. It's not the same."

His gaze, as cold as hers, held a superior amusement she found maddening. "It is the same. All peoples have traditions and heritages. Just different ones."

"Wrong," Piper retorted. "No ancestor of mine ran around sacrificing pigs and dropping jewels into volcanoes."

"No," he agreed sarcastically. "An ancestor of yours would have run around in a plaid skirt even if he was a man. He'd play on an instrument that looks like an octopus and sounds like a flock of starlings being tortured. For fun he'd try killing his fellow man with a broadsword. A truly illustrious forebear."

Piper's mouth assumed a dangerous angle. "Well, your illustrious forebears ran around beating on drums and scalping people."

"My point exactly," he said with infuriating calm. "If you look far enough back, all our ancestors seem a bit...quaint. The British, I believe, once painted themselves blue and worshiped mistletoe."

"Mr. Whitewater," Piper said, her patience at an end, "I think I'll go to the gate to wait for the plane. I don't need any history lessons, thank you."

She made a move to rise, but he put his hand over hers, pinning it firmly to the table. "You probably need a great many lessons, Miss Gordon. Because you keep looking down that pretty nose and not listening. The Scots don't use broadswords any more. But they still, on occasion, wear kilts and play bagpipes. It binds them to their past. The Hawaiians were forced to give up much of their past. They just want respect shown to the little they have left.''

Piper was shocked that he had the effrontery to touch her. The unwanted contact sent a furor of conflicting emotions racing through her. ''I'd like respect shown to *me,* Mr. Whitewater. I'd like to leave. Don't make a scene.''

His strong brown fingers curled around her tensed ones. The line appeared between his eyebrows again. When he spoke, false concern infused his voice. ''Your hand is freezing. Does reasonable talk make your blood run cold? If you can't win an argument, do you run away?''

For an instant the heat of his hand made hers feel even chillier than it was, then suddenly it began to warm, his heat blazing first through her flesh, then her blood. But she refused to give him the satisfaction of a struggle.

''I'm not the one using physical force to make my point,'' she said, her voice trembling with anger.

He lifted her hand slowly, turned it palm up, his thumb lightly caressing her knuckles. Her muscles stiffened.

''You call this force?'' he asked, stroking her palm. He shook his head, bemused. ''Such a cold hand. Such a tense one.'' He gave it a provocative squeeze. ''This isn't force. This is . . . friendly persuasion.''

She said nothing, only stared at him, resentment flashing in her eyes. He moved his hand so that it was palm to palm with hers, his fingers lacing intimately through her own.

What does he think he's doing? she wondered, her heart charging off at a gallop. Charming me? He's a handsome man, an arrogant man. Does he think all he has to do is touch me and I'll fall under his spell?

"If you have something sensible to say, say it," she muttered coldly. "But first let go of me."

Once more the hint of a smile played at the corner of his lips. His hand moved to surround hers once again, squeezing it as if to suggest that the two of them might be friends, perhaps something more. "We have a long way to travel together. We might as well be civilized."

He gave her a look that seemed perfectly sincere. His hand pulsed warmly against her own. But the eyes staring into hers didn't seem civilized in the least to Piper. Mystery, danger and cunning swam in their blue depths. She felt as if she had to strike out to defend herself.

"I was born civilized, Mr. Whitewater," she said. "You still seem to be learning the finer points of the process. But I'm a patient woman. If it upsets you that much not to have an audience, I'll stay. Just stop touching me. I'll hear you out."

The hand that gripped hers tensed. Fleetingly, displeasure clouded his face and the lines beside his mouth deepened. A new emotion glinted briefly in his eyes, and its power alarmed her. But it was gone almost as soon as it occurred, and she found herself staring at his mouth as it curved in that puzzling apparition of a smile.

"Touché, Miss Gordon," he said. He released her hand and picked up his coffee cup. "I won't forget my place again."

Piper quickly dropped her hand into her lap, clenching it so that the pulses in her fingers wouldn't throb so furiously. Her remark had been rude, but she would not apologize. She didn't think it had been ruder than his presumptions.

"I have," he said from between his teeth, "only two things to discuss with you. One is the necklace. It doesn't matter if you believe in its spiritual significance. It doesn't matter if I believe in it. It doesn't even matter if modern

Hawaiians do. The point is, Hawaiians still feel deeply about the spirits of their ancestors. This necklace was the property of one of those ancestors. Out of respect, it should be disposed of as he wished.''

''Oh, really,'' Piper said, clenching her fist harder. ''How could anybody know what he'd want? He's been dead almost two centuries.''

He shrugged. ''We can only go by what the documents about the necklace say.''

She tossed her head. ''Are people sure those documents are genuine?''

''They're real—as far as anybody can tell.''

''They're a mishmash,'' she countered irritably, looking away from him. ''They're partly in Portuguese and partly in Hawaiian and partly in Pidgin English, and the translation is terrible. They ramble on forever.''

''Have you read them all?'' Mockery played in his voice.

She flashed him a stormy glance. ''Of course not. They're unreadable.''

''You should try. Some of it's...amusing.'' His eyelids lowered lazily, as if he were remembering a private joke, and his lashes cast sharp shadows on his cheekbones.

''What's so funny?'' she challenged.

''Nothing. Read them. I said there were two things I wanted to discuss. The first was the necklace. Do you have any questions about that?''

''No,'' Piper replied shortly. ''What it comes down to is this—it doesn't matter if *anybody* believes the nonsense about it. We have to break it up and throw it away because somebody's ancestor *might* have believed in the ritual. Performing this idiocy is somehow a sign of respect.''

He shook his head in wry distaste. ''You've got the basic idea. What you don't have is the proper spirit.''

She gave him a baleful look. If there was a proper spirit, she doubted it would ever possess her. "What's the second thing you wanted to discuss?"

His face sobered. The frown line etched itself between his brows. He picked up the copy of *Gone with the Wind* and stared at the cover. In its foreground, Scarlet and Rhett smoldered. In the background, Atlanta burned.

Piper stared at him in surprise. His handsome face looked both puzzled and enigmatic. She raised her eyebrows in question.

"I'm in the seventh chapter," he said, frowning harder. "So far Scarlet's met only one man who has a lick of sense—Rhett Butler. So what's she do? She throws a vase at his head. Why? Why'd she have her heart set on that fool Ashley?"

His eyes met hers and sent an agitated tickle of sensation dancing down her spine. She made her expression as implacable as she could. "Ashley's a . . . a gentleman."

"And Rhett?" He cocked a skeptical eyebrow.

"And Rhett," she said, "Rhett . . . is not."

He shrugged. "She wants her own kind. I can understand that. A gentleman. That's what she wants?"

He gave the word "gentleman" a slightly contemptuous inflection and seemed to study her more intently than ever.

"Yes. No. It's . . . very complicated," she said in frustration. "Why are you reading that, anyway? Shouldn't you have a law book or something?"

"I've never had time to read it. It's a long flight to Hawaii and back. You've never made it before, have you?"

"How do you know?" she asked, suspicious.

He laid down the book. He looked her up and down, taking in her tailored suit, her smooth hair, her glinting earrings. "The same way I knew who you were when you walked in. Everything about you matches—and is expensive. Of superior quality—but not comfortable. What did you bring to read? A nice book on finance?''

She was glad she never blushed, because she had, indeed, brought a thick book on business management and finance. "What of it?" she asked.

He shrugged and glanced at his watch. "Nothing," he said, picking up his book again. "It's just that you're going to hate everything in about ten hours. Come on. It's time to fly."

He threw down a dollar and some change for his coffee and a tip, then picked up his carry-on bag and stood, slinging the strap over one wide shoulder. He drew her chair back and, despite her look of protest, took her carry-on bag as well.

When she stood, he linked his arm through hers. She was sure he meant it only as a gesture of politeness, but she thought she detected a hint of insolence in the movement.

She glanced up at his enigmatic profile, too conscious of the nearness of his powerful body. His eyes already seemed to be trained on some far horizon, his mouth set in a mixture of resignation and determination.

Piper's heart banged like a drum being beaten by a maniac. "I don't like this," she said as he began to propel her toward the gate. "I don't like this one bit."

His legs were long and she almost had to skip along on her high heels to keep up. He gave her elbow an encouraging squeeze, which didn't encourage her in the slightest. "Look on the bright side," he advised. "You and I get to go to Hawaii."

"I don't want to go to Hawaii with you," Piper said unhappily. The longer she spent in this man's presence, the more she wished she was back where she should be—in the quiet security of the jewelry store. "There *is* no bright side. Not one. My grandmother always said you were a fast-talking lying scalawag without an ounce of principle. I hate this. I really do.''

David Whitewater only smiled. This time there was no mistaking it. His mouth actually did turn up in something approaching mirth. The dimple deepened in his cheek and he cast her a taunting sidelong glance.

"If I'm such an unprincipled liar," he said, "why is your grandmother trusting me with you? Or more important, with her precious necklace?"

A chill ran through her. It was a question she had thought about. She drew herself up, trying to look as haughty and controlled as possible. "I suppose it's because she knows I can handle you," she said.

"Ha," said David Whitewater.

CHAPTER THREE

WHITEWATER, CURSE HIM, had been right. Piper hated everything—her seat, and especially the way she felt—before the flight was a quarter finished. They flew to Dallas, then boarded a jet that would be in the air eight hours, winging over the ocean to Hawaii.

Eloise didn't believe in spending money on such unnecessary luxuries as first-class seating. Piper and David were crammed into two small seats with scant leg room.

David gave Piper the window seat, but she didn't much like air travel and tried not to look out. When she did, all she saw was a turbulent cloudscape of hostile gray.

David had shed his jacket and lounged comfortably in his jeans and sweatshirt, reading *Gone with the Wind*. The stewardess, in a long blue-and-white Hawaiian dress, seemed to find him fascinating and kept stopping to see if he wanted a magazine, a pillow, a drink, a blanket. He smiled blandly on each occasion and told her he was fine.

Piper felt anything but fine, and took a drink to soothe her nerves. Instead the liquid seemed to sway in her stomach like nauseating poison. Her legs were cramped and her feet kept falling asleep. Her suit was uncomfortable and constricting; the book she had brought unreadable. The big plane began bucking storm winds from the moment it reached the Pacific, and each time it lurched, Piper felt both alarmed and sick.

She rented earphones from the stewardess and resigned herself to sit through both the mediocre in-flight movies.

The farther they flew, the worse the weather became and the more the plane pitched and vibrated. Piper tried not to imagine the sea, cold and tossing, beneath the clouds. The thought of crashing into it truly horrified her.

"I hate this," she muttered halfway through the first boring movie. The plane shook with an ominous series of bumps and shudders. A baby began to wail. In frustration she took off her earphones.

"Shhh," David Whitewater said, not looking up from his book. "The Yankees are coming. Does this woman ever realize what she really wants?"

"Why are you reading that?" Piper demanded. She was so bored, uncomfortable and nervous that even a conversation with Whitewater seemed a welcome distraction.

He gave her a short impatient glance. The jewel-blue of his eyes was as startling as ever. "Women love this book. I wanted to know why. Now I see. Scarlet never does one logical thing."

She sighed. She had forgotten how impossible he was. "Don't be sexist."

"I'm not sexist. I'm honest. It's a good book. It'd make a great movie."

"It *did* make a great movie," Piper retorted. "Where have you been? Living in a cave?"

"I grew up on a reservation," he said dryly. "It wasn't exactly the movie capital of the world."

"Everybody's seen *Gone with the Wind*," Piper protested grumpily. "Probably people living on Mars have seen *Gone with the Wind*. Penguins in Antarctica have probably seen *Gone with the Wind*."

"Bully for the penguins. I haven't. So if you'll excuse me, I'll read it. If you're bored, take a nap. Or watch the movie."

Offended, Piper once more put on her earphones. She couldn't sleep sitting up, but neither could she concentrate on the movie. How was a person supposed to concentrate? she thought irritably, when the plane tossed about like a bucking bronco and all she had for comfort or company was a smart-mouthed lawyer?

The movie limped to its pointless end. She tried listening to the plane's music channels, but they all sounded scratchy and metallic. Each time she shifted her position, her shoulder brushed David's; his shoulders were too wide for such narrow seats. She fidgeted.

He looked at her in mild annoyance.

"What's happening?" she asked sardonically, nodding at the book.

"Melanie's in...an interesting condition and Prissy doesn't know anything about birthing babies. This is good. Don't tell me you want to chat. I want to find out what happens."

"I don't want to chat," Piper muttered, then grimaced as the plane jerked and shivered again. "I just asked—" she winced as they hit another pocket of turbulence "—I just asked a civil question."

"You're also turning green," he said. "Maybe you should get up and walk around or something."

"I can't," she countered. "My legs are asleep. Besides, the Fasten Seat Belts sign is on. It's been on for three hours. Or haven't you noticed? This plane is bouncing around as if the gods are playing Ping-Pong with it."

He shrugged, which made his shoulder graze hers for the thousandth time. "Relax."

"I can't relax. We're pitching around over an *ocean*. If we crash, we'll drown. Or be eaten by sharks or marlins or whales."

"I don't think marlins or whales eat people. Except in Biblical instances. Is that what bothers you? That we're over the ocean?"

"Of *course* it bothers me. It should bother any sensible person."

"A sensible person doesn't think about it. A sensible person brings a good book. And wishes his seatmate would let him read it."

The plane wobbled again, and Piper bit her lip. She felt miserable and more than a little frightened. She stared straight ahead so she wouldn't have to look out the window at the swirling gray clouds that hid the treacherous sea. Tears stung her eyes and stubbornly she fought them back. Up until now, the only things in her life that had ever frightened her were snakes and lizards, which she seldom encountered in the city. She wasn't used to fear, and she hated it.

"A real white-knuckle flier," David said, shaking his head. Disgust tinged his voice. "You're just like my aunt when we flew over for my brother's wedding. Come here. This is the only thing that helped."

He pushed up the armrest that barely separated them and put his arm around her shoulders. She wanted to resist, but at the same moment the plane leapt and vibrated again. She shuddered, surrendered her willpower and lay her head against his shoulder, admitting that she felt wretched. For the moment it was altogether too easy to forget he was her family's enemy.

The plane lurched, and she squeezed her eyes shut. The crying baby screamed more loudly. Someone cried out to the stewardess that he was going to be sick.

Piper shut her eyes more tightly and burrowed more snugly against David. His arm tightened around her, pulling her nearer. "It's all right," he said. "I've got you."

She nodded and rested, exhausted, against him. It made no sense. She was just as vulnerable as before, the air was just as rough, the sea beneath them still as lethal. She didn't even like this man. But for some reason, she felt better, safer, within the shelter of his arm.

"I'm sorry," she murmured against his chest. He smelled warm and faintly spicy.

He nodded mechanically and pulled her closer as the plane dipped and danced again. He turned his concentration back to the book. "All in a day's work," he said, sounding bored.

"WAKE UP," said the low slightly raspy voice in her ear. "We're here."

She blinked in confusion. Her face rested against something warm and reassuringly solid. Her body felt secure, held by a live warm force that seemed absolutely dependable. Her legs, however, were so numb she barely felt them.

Raising her eyes, she was startled to see the wry curve of David Whitewater's mouth. A nice mouth it was, too, she thought, still disoriented: strong, sculpted and firm. She looked a bit higher and was jolted, as always, by the electric blue of his eyes.

She straightened, drawing away from him. "I don't believe it. When did I fall asleep?"

He took his arm from around her shoulders. She felt chilled, vulnerable without it.

"When we got out of the turbulence. About when Atlanta was burning."

"How long have I been asleep?"

"Long enough for Scarlet to cut up the drapes so she'd have something to wear to see Rhett. Resourceful. I admire that. Come on. Can you stand?"

Her muscles stiff, her legs unfeeling, she didn't protest when he grabbed their carry-on bags with one hand, then put his free arm around her and helped her hobble down the aisle. He glanced down disapprovingly at her high-heeled shoes. "Why do women put those things on their feet, anyway? Talk about savage customs."

"My grandmother taught me that one dresses like a lady when one travels," Piper muttered, leaning against him for support. "Oouf. Ouch."

"Your grandmother obviously never spent eight hours in a flying sardine can. Look, just take them off, okay?"

He set her on the arm of the nearest seat, bent and whisked off the offending shoes. He handed them to her and then, putting his arm around her once more, guided her down the aisle.

Barefoot, numb, limping, and supported by a smiling blue-eyed Sioux Indian, Piper arrived in Hawaii.

THE ISLAND OF OAHU was more beautiful than Piper had imagined, more beautiful than she *could* have imagined. As she stepped into the terminal, the very air seemed to embrace her; it was soft, welcoming, warm, and fragrant with the scent of leis.

Parts of the terminal were roofed but otherwise it was open; and for the first time in her life, Piper saw palm trees. In the distance Diamond Head rose beyond the soaring buildings of Honolulu. The sky was a lovely lavender blue. Beyond Diamond Head, a rainbow was fading softly away.

Piper stared, dazed and disbelieving. She had seldom been out of Nebraska, never farther from home than Chicago. All winter long she had looked upon the flat grayness of the Midwest, hungering for warmth and life and color. Now it surrounded her in lush abundance.

"Close your mouth—you'll swallow a fly," David told her as he wrestled their luggage into a cart.

"This is beautiful. This is wonderful," she said, inhaling the scent of tuber roses and carnations that filled the air.

"This is only the airport," David said sarcastically. "Save a little awe for the rest."

"But it's so strange. It feels different. Even the air is different—it feels so warm and free."

"Come on, Shoeless Lou, let's flag a cab and get to the hotel."

Piper had forgotten she was barefoot and carrying her shoes. She didn't care. Her severely tailored beige suit suddenly seemed like the drabbest and most confining of garments. She wanted to wear something colored like a rainbow and to pin real flowers in her hair.

In the cab, she could not keep from gaping at the sights of Honolulu. "That tree has coconuts on it," she said, pointing.

"Amazing," David said out of the corner of his mouth. He was trying to read his book again. "Perhaps it's a coconut tree."

"Oh, don't be so blasé," she told him. "*Look* at those flowers. What *is* that bush?"

"Bougainvillea. Settle down. Stop wiggling. You're distracting. I've got to finish this chapter."

"How can you read at a time like this? Look at that. There are orchids growing along the street. Orchids!"

"I've seen it. This is just the city, the touristy part. Settle down. I've got to find out if Rhett lends her the money to save Tara."

"What time is it—Hawaiian time?"

He frowned, the deep line carving itself between his dark brows, and glanced at his watch. "About seven-thirty. We gained four hours."

"Then the night's still young. What are we going to do tonight?"

He shut his book and gave her a cool stare. "I don't know what *you're* going to do. *I'm* going to see my brother and sister-in-law."

His answer jolted her. After his kindness on the plane, she had assumed they'd spend the evening together. In her delight over Honolulu, she'd somehow temporarily forgotten how deeply Eloise hated him and that she should hate him, too. "Oh. I didn't realize—"

"Look, I'd ask you to come, but it's nothing special. Just family stuff. We'll toss a couple of steaks on the grill, talk about old times. You wouldn't be interested."

She sat straighter, adjusted her crumpled skirt. She suddenly felt foolish holding her shoes. "Of course," she said, and slipped on first the right one, then the left.

He shrugged and rubbed his upper lip meditatively. "I mean, you could come if you wanted. My brother's an interesting guy. He runs a charter fishing service. My sister-in-law's nice. She works at the zoo. She's always got a baby hyena or an orphaned chimpanzee or something."

"I wouldn't dream of intruding," she said, lacing her fingers together in her lap and staring out the window. "I have things to do—"

"You wouldn't be intruding." Irritation edged his voice.

"No," she said, not looking at him. "Thank you very much, but no. We've spent all day together. I'm sure you need a break from my company as much as I need one from yours."

A moment of silence pulsed between them. "Right," he said at last. "Dead right."

ELOISE HAD RESERVED the most inexpensive rooms available in a rather expensive hotel, for, as she had told Piper wryly, there were no cheap hotels in Honolulu.

Piper's room did not face the ocean. It had a small balcony, but when she stepped out on it, she could see nothing except neighboring hotels.

She showered, washed her hair and blew it dry. She changed into a crisp blue-and-white seersucker suit and white leather sandals. Finally, she changed her earrings to ones of white pearl.

Piper's reflection in the mirror stared back at her somberly. She looked as she always looked: neat, tidy and smooth-haired. She carried herself as she always did, with an air of assurance she sometimes didn't feel. Her gray-blue eyes, however, were wary.

How did David Whitewater see her? she wondered. Did she perhaps look more moneyed than she was, a bit untouchable, perhaps even snobbish?

Or, she thought, maybe she didn't look aloof at all, just dull. The seersucker suit was expensive but, like all her clothing, conservative. Her short hair, her disdain of makeup other than lip gloss, suddenly seemed a bit too nononsense to her. Maybe everything about her was too orderly and understated.

An uptight Midwesterner, she thought critically, shaking her head at her reflection. Everything forthright, simple, tasteful—and boring.

This was vain and futile, she reprimanded herself. What did she care what the man thought? Eloise had raised her to be above such concerns. And besides that, he could be an extremely disagreeable man, and a sea of bad blood ran between them.

She changed her beige purse for a white one and, locking the door behind her, went out to explore. It was almost midnight Nebraska time, but she was restless and it was too late to call Eloise, who liked to be in bed by ten.

Piper felt odd. It was one of the few days in her life that she hadn't talked to her grandmother at least twice.

She went into the hotel's gift shop, looked at postcards and read the information on their backs. She bought a few to send to Eloise, Jeannie, and Harold and his wife, and tucked them into the pocket of her skirt.

She strolled the grounds, which were exquisite. There were so many kinds of nodding palms that she lost count, as well as beds of exotic flowers and a pond where flamingos dozed, their heads tucked beneath pink wings.

She finally headed toward the pale stretch of beach. The sand glittered in the moonlight and looked almost blue.

The waves rolled in, cresting with froth that shone a ghostly silver. She made her way across the sand carefully, as if she were treading on magic ground.

So this was the sea of which she had been so fearful, she thought, looking out into the darkness at its vastness. It gave her a strange tingling feeling. She had never been close to an ocean before.

The hiss and roar of the waves striking the sand, then retreating, was primitive and mystical, like the beating of a great wild heart.

She could not resist the impulse to take off her shoes and walk barefoot on the sand, which still radiated heat from the day's sun. She even dared get near enough the ocean to let its eddies wash over her toes, and was surprised at the warmth of the water. But she had grown up landlocked and knew nothing of the mysteries of the sea. She stayed at its very edge, uncertain of things like undertows and tides.

The sky was starless but luminously blue, curving down to meet the black sea at the horizon. Piper backed away from the foam of the waves and stood, just staring and listening to the surge and growl of the water.

No wonder the Greeks and Romans had believed there were gods in the sea, she thought. It was impossible to look upon so much power without feeling awe. She had always loved nature, but growing up in the heart of the city she'd had little chance to indulge that love. She had seldom seen anything wilder than a municipal park.

The breeze stirred her hair and rippled her skirt. She inhaled the warm salty air deeply and closed her eyes. I'm not really here, she told herself. I'll wake up back in Nebraska, where it's still winter. But if this is a dream, it's one I'll remember forever.

"What are you doing? Having a mystical experience?" The voice, as well as the taunting tone, were familiar. She whirled to see David standing behind her.

He, too, had changed clothes. His slacks were white, his knit shirt a muted blue or gray.

The breeze stirred his dark hair, making it flutter against his forehead. His hands were thrust casually into his pockets and he wore a lei of heavy white carnations and another of large yellow blossoms. The moonlight silvered his features, emphasizing his high cheekbones, the dark shadow of his lashes, the strong curve of his jaw.

"Oh," she said. Her heart began to pound with a rhythm as primal as the sea's. "I—I thought you were with your family."

He stared up at the moon as if bored. "I was. Josie's baby-sitting a lion cub. The little sneak ate our steaks. So we came to the hotel to eat. It's supposed to have a four-star restaurant. They thought maybe you'd want to join us for a drink. Supper, too, if you haven't had it."

"That's very kind of you," she said, careful to keep her voice even. "But I told you, I don't want to intrude."

He raised an eyebrow. "It's not kind of me, it's kind of Josie. She invited you. She nearly kicked me out the door for not bringing you along. Come on. It's not every day you get to meet a lion's stepmother."

She smiled slightly. "How did you know I was here?"

He shrugged and kept staring at the moon. "Two kinds of women stay in these hotels. One kind heads out to shop till she drops—and Wakiki stays open late to make sure it gets every last tourist dollar. The other kind takes moonlight strolls. I thought you'd be here."

He took her arm and began to walk her back to the hotel. She wished her pulses didn't leap so wildly at his touch. "Is that a compliment?" she asked doubtfully.

He shook his head. "I don't know. Maybe you just seem too swanky to shop along the strip."

She shot him a resentful glance. "I am not," she said, "swanky."

"Are those real pearls in your perfect little ears?"

"Yes, but they're not—"

"That tasteful little outfit you've got on probably cost enough to feed a family of four for a week."

"Not if they like to eat well."

"Where I came from, we didn't worry about eating well. We worried about eating."

"I refuse to feel guilty because my grandmother likes me to dress nicely," Piper said impatiently.

"I didn't ask you to feel guilty. I just said you were swanky. What is it your grandmother claims? That she's related to royalty?"

"Not royalty," Piper said, "just nobility."

"Just nobility," he practically snorted. "Barons and earls? She likes people to know her blood is bluer than that sky up there. She let me know that, too, in no uncertain terms. She and you are the elect. Unlike me."

Piper stopped and so did he. "Look. Maybe I should just go back to my room."

"Too aristocratic for my humble company?"

"Mr. Whitewater—"

"I love the way you say *Mr.* Whitewater. It's so condescending, yet so ladylike."

"Why do you insist on seeing me as a snob?"

"I don't. Exactly."

"What's that mean?"

He gave a harsh sigh. "I don't know. Maybe you're too perfect. Even when you got off the plane, sleepy, barefoot, rumpled, you looked . . . perfect. It's annoying. It's unnatural. Doesn't your hair ever get messy? Has your nose ever been smudged?" He paused, his glance dwelling on her mouth. "Does your lipstick ever smear?"

She looked up at him in perplexity.

"I mean it," he said, his eyes locking with hers. "You're barefoot in the sand. You should be . . . windswept or something. But there you just stand, holding your perfect little shoes in your perfectly manicured hand, not one hair out of place. It's probably impossible to smear your lipstick."

His dark hair stirred in the breeze, and she had the absurd desire to smooth it back into place. She could smell the sweet and spicy scents of the flower leis.

"We could see," he said, his voice low. He stepped closer to her. He took the yellow lei from his neck and settled it around hers.

"There," he said, staring at her mouth again. "Josie got on my case because I didn't give you flowers. It's a tradition when you arrive in Hawaii. So's a welcoming kiss. An excellent opportunity to experiment."

The flowers felt cool and delicate next to her flesh; they filled her nostrils with intoxicating fragrance. Her heart pounded again. It pounded harder as he took her face between his hands and tilted it upward toward his.

"So," he said softly, "here's to scientific inquiry." He bent his head, and his lips, warm, firm and expert, met hers.

Piper's heart felt as if it would fly from her body in astonishment and mixed emotion. One of his hands lingered, gentle yet sure against her face. The other moved to ruffle her silken hair. The mouth against hers was seductively insistent and felt as warm and magical as the tropical air that embraced her. Almost against her will, her lips parted beneath his as his touch grew more intimate, more demanding, more magical still.

The sea crashed and hissed, the scent of flowers drugged her, and she could feel the strong steady beat of his heart against her breasts. She knew she should draw away, but could not.

But neither did she allow herself to respond. His nearness filled her with a strange foreign craziness she didn't understand. She hadn't wanted him to kiss her; he was too different from her, too dangerous. But now, perversely, with his lips hot and questing against hers, she liked his difference and danger.

She forced herself to stand still, not to touch him, and in spite of the beating of her pulses, she made herself as unyielding as a statue. She was a woman who was used to being in control, and it alarmed her that he made her feel precisely the opposite.

He drew back. His long-lashed eyes looked almost black in the moonlight, and he stared down at her, studying her for a long moment. His hand fell away from her hair and settled companionably on her shoulder. The one-cornered hint of a smile crooked his mouth.

"Nope," he said irreverently, gazing at her lips. "Not even a smear." He looked at her hair, and the dimple in his cheek deepened. "And every hair still in place. You're not human."

She took a deep breath. She remembered Eloise's words: *Never forget who you are. And never forget what that man did to us.* Resentment flooded through her in a cold wave.

"Don't think I enjoyed that," she said frostily. "I didn't."

He stepped away from her, putting his hands in his pockets. He shrugged. "It was okay. Don't worry. My curiosity's satisfied. It won't happen again."

"It certainly *won't*," Piper said, avoiding his arm when he reached out to take hers.

He looked unconcerned, almost bored again. He lifted a shoulder as if her reaction made no difference to him. "Rest easy. You're not my type. I prefer Native American women. Somebody I'd have something in common with. You're too much like your grandmother. Hardheaded." He gave a curt nod of emphasis, almost to himself. "Besides, we have to watch it. The ritual demands that you and I stay celibate while we carry it out."

"*What?*" Piper demanded, shocked at his words.

"Celibate," he repeated. "No sex. None. It's *kapu*. Forbidden. I told you that you should have read the whole document. No, I'm afraid you and I just peaked, sexually speaking."

He began walking toward the hotel again and she followed, hurrying to keep up with his long-legged stride. "You're completely intolerable, you know. Has anyone ever told you that?"

He cast her a sidelong look. "Usually at least once a day."

"It's nothing to be proud of."

"It's not?" he mocked. "Damn!"

"Look, Mr. Whitewater—"

"I love the way you say that. I really do. Be careful. I might kiss you again."

"You will *not*. I'm going to my room. Give my thanks to your brother and his wife, but—"

"No," he said with surprising firmness. "Stop and have a drink. Aaron's got some interesting things to say about your volcano goddess. You might want to hear him out."

"She's not *my* volcano goddess. I don't believe in her."

He turned, looking down at her with a measuring stare. "I don't, either," he said with his vexing half smile. "But who knows? This place seems to get to you. You might change your mind."

"Impossible," Piper said, shaking her head in determination.

The dimple played its shadowy game in his cheek. "Too rational? Like your grandmother again, eh?"

Piper, by his side, didn't bother to answer. She felt full of strange emotions that were not rational at all.

CHAPTER FOUR

PIPER FOUND David Whitewater's older brother, Aaron, to be almost as disturbing a man as David. When he stood to greet her, she saw that he was even taller than David, and the set of his mouth convinced her that mockery ran in the family.

Josie Whitewater was tall, slim, and intelligence gleamed in her eyes. She had a tumble of dark red curls and her cheekbones were burnished by the sun and spangled with faint freckles. Piper was impressed by the obvious depth of affection between the couple, the sense that they not only loved, but genuinely liked and respected each other.

"Tell her about Pele," Josie said to her husband. Aaron was drinking a scotch on the rocks. Piper and Josie had mai tais, and David drank black coffee.

Aaron's eyes, unlike David's, were dark. They settled on Piper, and she had the eerie feeling he could see into her soul if he wanted.

"What you're caught up in is strange. It's not typical. I told David that from the first."

Josie, looking thoughtful, nodded. David hardly seemed to be listening to his brother. He reached over and rumpled Josie's hair affectionately. The gesture made Piper's heart give a painful jump of pleasure, although at the same time it made her feel lonely, an outsider.

"The business of your talking to three priestesses is also strange," Aaron Whitewater said, sipping his scotch.

"Why?" Piper asked. She found herself fascinated by the similarities between the brothers; their height, their broad shoulders, their tawny complexions and dark hair. They were both men who were sure of themselves and looked on the world with irreverence.

Yet they were different, as well. David was leaner, more restless, more complex. The intense blue of his eyes bespoke of the intensity within him. He could seem relaxed, almost lazily calm on the surface, but full of fire that sometimes smoldered, sometimes blazed. She also somehow sensed that they viewed life differently. Aaron, she felt, looked upon the world as a place tinged with mystery, but David saw one constructed on the rigid principles of logic and justice. David might be the one fighting for Native American rights, but it was Aaron who seemed more Indian, both in appearance and outlook.

"First," Aaron said, turning his glass thoughtfully, "the Hawaiians had many gods. Pele wasn't the most important. But her influence has hung on. Maybe because she's the most visible."

"And most impressive," Josie added, smiling at her husband. "It's hard to be on the Big Island and not believe in her—a little."

Aaron nodded. "She's also an ancestral goddess," he said. "That means certain families trace their lineage back to her. When the descendents of Pele—like your chief—died, their bones were carried to the volcano, to the source of life itself. It was how things were done."

Piper was conscious of David's eyes on her, watching her reaction to these beliefs, which were so foreign to her. She was careful to keep her face politely impassive.

"Hawaii has always had its kahunas—its experts, people with insight into the supernatural," Aaron went on. "A kahuna could be a man or a woman. Some were said to be sorcerers."

Piper nodded. "Like the Portuguese sailor. The one who made the necklace."

"Right," Aaron said. "But these rituals aren't really part of the Hawaiian native religion. In fact, some don't like to call it 'religion' at all—that gives the idea it was formal, set down in stone. It wasn't."

"It's more personal," David said, still watching her. "For those who believe."

"A person's relationship to Pele," Josie explained, "isn't written down in rules and regulations. It's from the heart. It's private. Spiritual."

"And the believers—the true believers—don't discuss it with you or me," Aaron said. "We're haoles—foreigners."

"And *malihini*," Josie added. "Newcomers."

"What are you saying?" Piper asked. Uneasy currents started to course along her nerves.

"He's saying," David muttered out of the side of his mouth, "that the ritual is something that the Portuguese made up."

"I'm also saying," Aaron added, "that there are people around, dressing up in red, chanting and calling themselves priests or priestesses. But too many are like some of the preachers you see on TV—they're in it to look important and make a buck."

Piper frowned in consternation. "But . . ." she said, then didn't know how to finish the sentence.

David spoke, his voice cynical. "Aaron means that people who talk a lot about Pele usually don't know much about her. And those who know, don't talk much. At least not to the likes of you and me."

"I don't understand," Piper said, shaking her head. "Then to whom are we supposed to talk? Somebody who's just acting like a priestess for show? This gets more senseless all the time."

David's phantom smile hovered at the corner of his mouth. "Isn't she cute?" he said to Aaron. "The way she says 'whom'? Everything she does is so perfect."

"Be nice," Josie said, and gave him a playful pinch. "Or I'll feed you to the lion."

"I checked with the Hawaiian Cultural Bureau," Aaron said, turning to Piper. "They're careful about this sort of thing. They've got three women lined up for you. Whether they're actually priestesses is one question. Whether they'll tell you anything of consequence is another."

Piper felt the long trip and all the changes of the day catching up with her. Her head began to ache. She pushed her drink away and placed her hand against her forehead, leaning her elbow on the table.

"I don't understand this," she said grimly. "I'm supposed to be fulfilling the rules of a religion that nobody wants to call a religion. Anybody who'll talk to me doesn't understand it. Anybody who understands it won't talk to me. All because some old fraud of a deserter made up a bunch of mumbo jumbo. And *I* have to throw away something worth fifty thousand dollars."

"Well," Aaron Whitewater said philosophically, "if life were logical, it wouldn't be interesting. But Dave doesn't think so. He'd like it all logical."

David, silent, only glanced at his brother, lifting his eyebrow wryly.

"It does seem strange," Josie said, giving Piper a sympathetic nod. "Aaron got the feeling that the bureau wasn't too happy about it, either. That it's a strange case."

Piper looked at her questioningly.

Josie spread her fingers in a helpless gesture. "He just gets ... feelings," she said. "We've learned to trust them." She and Aaron exchanged a look that seemed filled with private meanings.

"It's the law, and that's that," David stated with finality.

"I wouldn't mind if my grandmother just had to give it back and it went to a museum," Piper said, her hand still pressed to her forehead. "I wouldn't mind if they sold it and used the money to help people. But to simply destroy it seems so *foolish*. I just don't understand."

Nobody said anything for a moment. The others, she felt with embarrassment, did understand.

"You're tired," David said, his voice cool and slightly harsh. "I'll take you to your room. Come on."

She nodded wearily and said goodbye to Aaron and Josie. "None of this makes sense," she said when she and David entered the elevator. She leaned back against the polished wooden wall and shut her eyes in fatigue.

"It's simple," David returned with the same chill harshness as before. "You're being asked to pay a little respect to somebody else's beliefs."

She set her mouth at a cynical angle. "Fifty thousand dollars should be worth more than 'a little respect.' It ought to be worth a perfectly ridiculous amount of respect. My grandmother ought to be the most respected person in these islands."

"Does it always come down to money?" he asked.

She opened her eyes. He was staring at her with an intensity that made her yearn to turn away, to flee, but there was nowhere to go. She raised her chin a trifle higher.

"Yes," she said sarcastically. "All I care about is money. And I'm so perfect and my blood is so blue I can be as snobbish as I like, because I *am* actually better than anyone else, especially you. There. I'll say it, so you can finally stop."

"You're so sure of yourself," he scoffed. "Some day somebody's going to come along and shake you out of your safe narrow little existence."

The elevator doors groaned open. Piper flashed him a rebellious look. She had known him only slightly more than twelve hours, and already he had shaken her safe narrow little existence as powerfully as an earthquake.

"Maybe some day," she said, stepping into the hall, "somebody will come along and inject some courtesy into *your* life." He stepped out with her.

"Not likely," he said with his superior smirk. "I'm a lawyer. It's my job to annoy people."

He stayed by her side, and when she drew her key from her purse, he took it and opened her door. When his fingers brushed hers, she felt them tingle as if they had contacted a live wire.

"If your job is to be annoying," Piper said, taking the key back, careful not to touch him, "you've attained absolute perfection. Congratulations. And good night."

"Good night, Miss Gordon. I'll see you in the morning. We have to see a priestess—more or less—and throw away some pearls."

She looked up at him, saw the smugness of his smile and the amused fire in his eyes. She remembered, fleetingly and with a pang, how warm, certain and magical his lips had felt against hers. She thrust the thought away as forcefully as if it were a draft of poison.

"I think I hate you, Mr. Whitewater," she said sweetly.

"Hate away," he said. "You won't be the first."

THE NEXT MORNING they took a taxi to the outskirts of Honolulu. Piper was restless. She had tried to telephone Eloise at both her private numbers, but got no answer.

She knew better than to phone Aunt Jeannie. Jeannie was terrified of long-distance calls, believing they had been invented solely to convey news of disaster. Piper would have to spend the entire conversation assuring Jeannie that nothing was wrong. Harold's home line was busy when she tried to call, and so was his business phone. She could reach nobody in the family.

Now, sitting beside David in the cab, Piper tried to avoid speaking to him as much as possible without being blatantly rude. She wore a pale blue linen shirtwaist dress with matching blue shoes and blue topaz earrings. She held her pale blue handbag firmly on her lap and stared out the window so that she wouldn't have to look at him.

David lounged beside her, his long legs encased in wheat-colored jeans. He wore cowboy boots and a chest-hugging yellow T-shirt with green lizards that glowered out at the world. He also had sunglasses, which, oddly, made him look more Indian. Piper supposed it was because they hid his jewel-blue eyes.

He sat, legs crossed, reading. "Damn," he said in irritation. "Scarlet's going to marry her sister's boyfriend. This woman stops at nothing. *Nothing*."

Piper darted him a disapproving glance. "She does what she has to do to save her family," she said, turning back to the window. "That's all."

"My," he said sarcastically, "we're touchy this morning. Why can't you talk nicely—the same way you look? I notice everything matches again. And not a wrinkle to be seen. How do you do it? Do elves come at night and iron everything for you?"

She shot him another displeased look. "You're the one who keeps talking about respect. We're going to see a priestess. I dressed for the occasion. You, unfortunately, seem to be dressed to rope steers."

"This is Hawaii," he said, not looking up from his book. "People hang loose. Besides, I talked to her on the phone this morning. She said not to dress up."

"Then why didn't you tell me?" Piper asked, nettled.

"Why didn't you ask?" He returned with aggravating calm. She didn't bother to answer.

The cab pulled up before a tiny squarish pink house with a coconut tree in the front yard. A rusted tricycle was parked across the sidewalk. A trio of sparrows hopped through the trimmed grass.

The house didn't look in the least like the dwelling of a priestess, but Piper felt a quiver of apprehension. When David took her arm to guide her up the walk, she didn't object.

He knocked at the screen door and took off his sunglasses. A child, a little girl of about four, came to the door. She had long curly black hair and she stared up at David suspiciously.

"We've come to talk to Mrs. Mary Lilola," David said.

The child examined him with even greater suspicion, then turned and, without ceremony, yelled, "Grandma!"

Piper clutched her purse, her heart beating faster. She had a sudden urge to bolt back to the waiting cab.

A woman of about sixty came to the door. She was tall, broadly built, and her short black hair was streaked with gray. She wore white slacks, a green cotton sweater, gold-rimmed glasses, and no makeup. Her dark gaze was steady. She did not smile.

"Mrs. Lilola," David said, "I talked to you this morning. I'm Whitewater. On business for the Cultural Bureau. This is Piper Gordon. She's brought the necklace that was connected with your family back to the islands."

The woman held a burning cigarette. She took a long drag, regarded them, exhaled, then opened the door. "Come in," she said. "Would you like something to eat or drink?"

"No, thank you," Piper started to say, but David discreetly elbowed her.

"A cup of coffee would be fine," he said, and gave Piper a sidelong look that told her to let him handle the situation.

Mary Lilola gave him a curt nod. "Sit down," she said, nodding at a well-worn flowered couch, before she turned and padded into the kitchen.

Piper settled onto the small couch and looked about the living room warily. The little girl lay stretched on the floor dressing a blond Barbie doll. Ignoring Piper and David, she hummed along to the country-and-western music tinkling from the radio.

A coffee table before the couch held a vase of red bougainvillea blossoms and a copy of the Honolulu newspaper. The couch was small, and she was overly conscious of David's nearness. She could feel the closeness of his arm; his muscular shoulder grazed her softer one, and she sensed the warmth of his long thigh next to hers.

She tried to ignore the feeling of power, pure and live, that radiated from him. Her eyes rested on a strange but compelling painting that hung on an opposite wall, and she forced herself to study it.

In dramatic reds, golds and blacks, the picture was of an imposingly handsome Hawaiian woman wearing a crown of red feathers. Her eyes reflected the glow of fires, and behind her loomed a mountain bathed in the glare of red. Somehow the painter had made it seem as if a river of fire ran from the mountain and became part of the woman's flowing hair. It was a hypnotic picture, disturbingly so, especially those solemn fiery eyes.

Piper glanced uneasily at David, who had followed her gaze. He nodded at the picture. "Madam Pele," he said. "And Aaron says people respect her enough to call her *madam*. Red's her color—the color of fire."

Piper stared again at the mysterious glowing eyes, the haughty set of Pele's mouth. She swallowed nervously. The little girl on the floor fastened a skirt on her doll and hummed along with "The Tennessee Waltz."

Mary Lilola returned from the kitchen, carrying a tray with coffee, cream, sugar and a plate of cookies. She set it on the table in front of them. "Help yourself," she said, still unsmiling. She took a cup and sat in a rocking chair. She crossed her legs and stared at David.

"You're not Hawaiian," she said bluntly.

"No, ma'am. I'm half Sioux Indian. I work for the Native American Legal Claims Organization. They've entrusted me with this project, with the approval of the Cultural Bureau."

"I've worked with the Cultural Bureau," Mary Lilola said. "They want me to talk to you about the necklace. I know nothing about it."

Piper spoke up. "It's supposed to have belonged to a chief on the Big Island. His name was Pikue—or something like that. Are you one of his descendents?"

The woman sipped her coffee. "Distantly," she said vaguely.

"Mrs. Lilola," David said, picking up his coffee cup, "documents that came with the necklace say it was supposed to be disposed of in a certain way when the chief died."

She shrugged. "If that's what it says, then it must be so."

"The necklace is very valuable, Mrs. Lilola," Piper said a bit desperately. "Are you sure the family wouldn't rather keep it, put it on display in a museum somewhere?"

The woman shrugged again. "It's not for me to say. What should be done should be done."

An awkward silence settled over them. The little girl looked up and asked if she could go outside and ride her tricycle. Mary Lilola nodded. The child ran outside, slamming the screen door behind her.

"Mrs. Lilola," David said. "The documents say that before the necklace is to be disposed of, we're to talk to three priestesses of Pele. The Cultural Bureau gave me your name. And you agreed to see us.''

The woman set down her cup. She gave him an enigmatic smile. "Only because I am . . . curious.''

Piper wiggled in frustration. "*Are* you a priestess?'' she asked.

"I know something about the old ways,'' Mrs. Lilola replied with her same maddening vagueness. "What is it you're supposed to talk about?''

"I . . . I don't even know,'' Piper said, making an ineffectual gesture. "We're supposed to talk to you and then go where there's white sand and throw some pearls—pearls from the necklace—into the ocean.''

The woman shook her head. "Pearls? They didn't come from here.''

"The necklace was made by a Portuguese sailor,'' David said. "In all likelihood, he brought the pearls from Tahiti. And I think, Mrs. Lilola, you're supposed to talk with us about Pele.''

"I know nothing about Pele and pearls. What is it you want to know?''

"Anything,'' Piper said. Out of politeness, she forced herself to take a sip of coffee. "I don't know anything about Pele at all. Is that her?'' She nodded at the painting of the woman with the fiery eyes.

Mrs. Lilola glanced at the picture, then studied Piper. "She takes many forms. Sometimes a young woman. Sometimes an old one. Sometimes she's fair. Sometimes she's dark. And she has a little white dog.''

"She supposed to have created the islands?'' David said, trying to encourage the woman to talk more freely.

She acknowledged the statement with a dubiously raised eyebrow. "Volcanoes created the islands. First Kauai. Then Oahu here, then the others. Last the Big Island.''

"And," David prompted, "some say Pele's fires still burn on the Big Island. On Mauna Loa."

Her face was impassive. "Fires still burn on Mauna Loa. Yes."

"And there are people who believe Pele might still want this necklace?" Piper asked.

"There might be such people," Mrs. Lilola said, her dark eyes trained with uncomfortable steadiness on Piper's face.

"What I don't understand," Piper said, "is why we throw part of the necklace into the sea."

The woman shrugged again. "For a time Pele owned the sea. For a time she was married to one of its gods. I don't know why. You must do it because that is what the papers tell you to do."

"Mrs. Lilola," David said, "anything you could tell us about Pele will be of help."

"She's said to live in the crater on the Big Island. She and her sisters."

"Sisters?" Piper asked.

"Her sisters. Her helpers. They're called the Cloud Holders."

"The Cloud Holders," Piper repeated, taken by the name.

Mary Lilola looked at Piper a long time, then turned to stare at David. Piper was discomfitted, but David met the scrutiny with his own cool gaze.

Mary Lilola seemed to relent a bit. She looked at Piper again and said, "I'll tell you a story about love."

Love? Piper thought. Why had the woman examined them so intently then decided to speak of love?

Once more Piper became overly conscious of David's body so near hers. She tried to shift away, but the couch was too small. Her shoulder brushed his, and her thigh only pressed his more intimately.

The woman nodded. "Once Pele wanted someone to bring her a prince that she loved. It was a long journey, dangerous. Her youngest sister, Hiiaka, went. And Pele warned her, 'Don't kiss him. He is mine.'

"After much danger, Hiiaka came to the prince's village. But he was dead. A sorcerer had killed him.

"Now Pele had given Hiiaka some of her power, her mana, to protect her. Hiiaka went to the prince's body, and using this power, she brought him back to life. This took a long time.

"Back home, Pele grew angry waiting. She set loose her fire and burned Hiiaka's favorite grove of flowering trees. When Hiiaka came home and saw what Pele had done, she wept. And this prince, seeing her weep, kissed her, for he had come to love her.

"Pele's other sisters saw this and told. Pele pretended not to care. She said, 'Mouths were made for kissing.'

"But Pele took her fires and killed the man she had wanted. And Hiiaka wept that he had tasted death twice, and Pele learned all that had happened.

"Then Pele softened, and for the second time the prince was restored to life. But this time he was Hiiaka's alone to kiss."

"And?" Piper asked, fascinated in spite of herself.

"And," Mary Lilola said with finality, "that is the story of Hiiaka, the youngest of the Cloud Holders. Pele can destroy. She can also create. *He e'epa ke aloha, he kula'ilua.*"

Piper looked at her in puzzlement.

For the first time the woman smiled. It was a small smile and a knowing one. "Love is peculiar, it pushes in opposite directions."

"I DON'T KNOW what to make of that," Piper said, when they were back inside the cab. She was still rattled by the experience. "Such a strange story."

"I didn't much like it," David said, staring into his book again. "The women got all the glory. The prince just kept falling over dead."

"What did she mean, love pushes in opposite directions?"

David shrugged. "Just what she said, I guess. Love can destroy—or create."

"I think there's more to it," Piper said, frowning. "I think it means love can transform, too. Or that there's a good kind of love and a bad kind." She glanced at him, his interest apparently absorbed by the book. "Are you going to be reading that thing the whole time we're in Hawaii?"

He gave a sharp sigh and closed it. "Apparently not while you're around, my little chatterbox. Look, when we get back to the hotel, get into your bathing suit and we'll take care of the pearls. Then we'll have about enough time to grab a bite to eat before we head for the Big Island."

"Bathing suit?" Piper asked, frowning harder than before. "Why?"

"How do you think we're going to get those pearls in the water? That I'd paddle you out in a war canoe?"

"Well," Piper said, unsettled, "I thought we'd take a boat or something, yes."

"No," he said firmly. "We don't need any witnesses. You'll do it alone. Except for me."

A quiver of apprehension tingled through her. "But...but I'm not a good swimmer. Really. And I've never swum in an ocean before."

"Don't worry. I swim fine. I'll take care of you."

I'll bet, Piper thought darkly.

"I CAN'T WATCH THIS," she said, turning her face away. She sat down on the bed, shielding her eyes. She wore a simple one-piece black bathing suit, a black terry cover-up and black thongs.

David was in a pair of white trunks and his same yellow T-shirt. He held the necklace and a pair of metal snips. "You should watch. Just to make sure I don't pull anything funny. That I don't switch the pearls on you. Here goes."

Piper grimaced and forced herself to watch. There were eight irregular white pearls in the necklace. One by one he snipped them free. Then, standing over her desk, he pried them from their crude settings.

"It makes me sick," Piper said, and turned away again. She couldn't bear seeing the necklace destroyed, its handiwork undone bit by bit. It was also disconcerting to have a man built like David Whitewater standing in her room with so few clothes on.

She slipped him a resentful glance. His legs were long, bronzed and extremely well-muscled, his stomach flat and his hips firm. Put a sarong on him, she thought grimly, and he'd look like one of those bronzed beachboy gods on the local postcards—except of course, for his blue eyes.

"Give me a handkerchief, will you?" he asked. "I forgot to bring one."

She rose reluctantly, opened a drawer and handed him a perfectly pressed handkerchief. He took it, shaking his head in displeasure. "This won't do. It's white. It doesn't match your...ensemble." He glanced pointedly at her black bathing suit and cover-up.

"What's that got to do with it?" she asked, crossing her arms impatiently. "Why does it bother you that my clothes match? Am I breaking some law? And *what* are you doing?"

He poured the pearls into the handkerchief and wrapped them tightly. "Making sure these are safe. I'll carry them until we get to the water." He thrust the packet into the waistband of his trunks. He put the rest of the mutilated necklace into his briefcase and locked it. "And this," he said, "goes back into the hotel safe until we leave. Ready?"

She felt another tremor of nervousness. She had promised Eloise to save a piece of the olivine. How was she going to do so, if David kept such tight guard on the necklace?

"I can't believe I'm really doing this," she grumbled. "I really can't."

She thrust on her sunglasses and threw her beach bag carelessly over her shoulder. "All right," she said with a toss of her head. "Come on, Mr. Whitewater. Let's go throw away a fortune."

He looked her up and down, from the smooth sweep of her satiny legs to the perfect neatness of her hair.

He gave her his most cryptic smile.

CHAPTER FIVE

SINCE THEY HAD LEFT Mary Lilola's, rain had fallen once and now it threatened to fall again.

The beach was not deserted, but neither was it crowded. The ocean stretched gray and choppy beneath an ominously gray sky.

The boom and sigh of the waves sounded more sinister to Piper than they had the night before. She and David picked the most deserted spot on the beach, and she quickly spread out her black-and-gray beach towel. Then she fussed about for her sunscreen lotion and other supplies.

Unpleasant thoughts swam through her mind: sharks and poisonous jellyfish and stingrays and moray eels and electric eels and giant squids and pinching lobsters and clams that would snap shut on toes, severing them. She licked her lips nervously.

"Come on," David said impatiently, pulling off his T-shirt. A ray of sun that had pierced the cloud cover gleamed on the dark ropy muscles of his arms and back, on the smooth expanse of his chest. The breeze tossed his dark hair across his forehead, and he'd taken off his sunglasses to reveal the disconcerting blueness of his eyes.

Oh, go pose for a calendar, Piper thought uncharitably. It wasn't enough she had to go into an ocean teeming with slimy things, she had to do it with Whitewater, who just happened to look like a half-naked Adonis.

She thinned her lips and shed her beach coat, kicking off her thongs. "I'm putting on some sunscreen first," she said, trying to play for as much time as possible.

"Look," he said, putting a hand on his hip, "we're not going to be out there long enough for you to worry about the sun."

"It's the safe thing to do, and I'm doing it," Piper argued. She took her sunglasses off and began to smooth the lotion on her face and chest. She sat on the beach towel and stroked it onto her arms and shoulders, then struggled to reach her back.

"Here," David growled, kneeling behind her and taking the bottle. "Lord, even your leftover tan's perfect. You're one of those people who's one color all over. Like a paint sample."

Piper turned her head to give him an unappreciative glance. He was rubbing the lotion onto her back with deep brisk strokes. "I do not," she said between her teeth, "look like a paint sample."

"No?" he said sarcastically. "Well, you do. Creamy beige or something." He moved in front of her and made her stretch her legs.

"Don't," she objected as his strong hands massaged the lotion into her calves and shins with long silky movements. "I can do it myself."

"You're too slow," he said, and began rubbing her thighs. "I'm a man who likes to get things done."

He was getting things done all right, Piper thought in consternation, watching the lean brown hands massaging her thighs. Her legs tingled clear up to her hips and she felt as if flying fish sported in the pit of her stomach.

"Roll over," he ordered, and when she didn't obey, he simply took her by the shoulders and turned her over himself. Piper didn't give him the satisfaction of arguing. She lay, her chin on her hands, staring unhappily at the tossing ocean.

David's hands slowed, moving a bit too caressingly over the backs of her thighs. "You have nice muscle tone," he informed her. "I love these spandex suits. They tell no lies."

He gave her an irreverent pat on the buttocks. "Come on."

Reluctantly she stood, looked out at the sea again and bit her lip. "I . . . don't know how to do this."

He stared down at her with amusement. "Look," he said, "pretend we're having a good time. I know it takes a lot of imagination, but just try to make it seem natural. Here. Take my hand."

He reached out, his strong hand capturing hers. She found herself staring at this half-naked man of bronze against a cloudy gray sky, dark hair stirring in the breeze. At first, he had his infuriating ghost of a smile, but slowly, as he looked down into her face, it died.

"Come on," he said with surprising kindness, and started toward the frothing waves, drawing her behind him.

The sand was cold and damp beneath her feet, the sea air warm and salty. She pulled back in apprehension when the water surged first over her ankles, then halfway to her knees. She balked.

David's hand tightened around hers. "Come on," he ordered.

Piper stumbled more deeply into the waves. The ocean seemed to swarm at her like an enemy, first pushing her back toward the shore, then pulling her more hopelessly into its depths.

She looked down in panic, trying to keep her footing, but she could no longer see her feet. Again a wave pushed her back, hard, toward the shore. The sand beneath her feet angled down sharply. She knew that in a few more steps she would be over her head. Fearfully she looked out at the horizon. It stretched gray as far as she could see, nothing but water, water, water.

David was already in almost to his waist and seemed perfectly surefooted against the buffeting of the waves. "Come on," he repeated, inexorably drawing her toward him.

Now the swaying water came almost to her chest. Droplets spattered her face, and the current seemed intent on knocking her feet from beneath her. Another wave crashed nearby; it stung her eyes and rained on her parted lips.

"Ugh!" she muttered, shaking her head.

"What's wrong?" David asked. "Come on—stop fighting it."

"It's *wet*," Piper almost spat, trying to shake the water from her eyes.

"It's the ocean," he said in disgust.

"It's salty," she said, affronted by the stinging in her eyes, the withering taste on her tongue.

"It's supposed to be salty."

Once more she scanned the hostile gray horizon, looking out over the heaving water that threatened to swallow her. "It's too big," she wailed.

"It's supposed to be big," David muttered impatiently. "If it wasn't big, it wouldn't be the damned ocean."

Another wave struck her, and as she staggered, she saw flashes of silver moving around her, driving toward the shore. She screamed. "Whitewater! There are fish here! One touched me!"

She tried to dodge the glimmering school of fish and lost her footing as the next wave struck. The shock almost made her release his hand as she was hurled backward and sucked down. She swallowed a mouthful of salty water, and David hauled her up, coughing and shaking like a wet puppy.

He took her into his arms and stared down at her sodden hair, her shocked and confused face. "Look, haven't you ever seen those movies where the girl runs into the ocean, dives in and swims out a little? That's all you have to do.''

She squinted up at him with stinging eyes. She resented the laughter twitching at the corner of his mouth and she resented having to rely on his superior strength. But paradoxically, she was grateful he was there, tall and strong and stubborn enough to resist the irresistible pull of the ocean.

Piper realized she had put one arm around his neck and that she probably intended to keep it there. She sputtered, trying to clear her throat. "I never *saw* an ocean until last night," she said. "I'm from Nebraska, remember?"

"Look," he said, tightening his arm around her waist, "think of this as Nebraska. Only wetter and saltier and bigger and with more fish. Relax."

"I can't relax," Piper said. "I've never swum in anything except a swimming pool."

"What?" he demanded, frowning. "Not even a lake? A river?"

"No," she protested. "Never. My grandmother never allowed it. She said it was too dangerous. Can't we just drop the pearls here?"

"No," he said, shaking his head, "We're hardly in the water yet. We've got to get farther out. Just hang on to me. But first take the pearls."

He dug into the waistband of his trunks and offered her the sodden packet. Piper shook her head. If he was going to swim farther out, she intended to hang on to him with both arms. She locked them obstinately about his neck. The ocean, like a great gray treacherous beast, wanted to pick her up and hurl her back toward the shore, pull her underwater, then suck her out to sea.

"You keep them. I can't hold them. And I don't have any pockets," she said. She intended to have some say in this matter; Whitewater wasn't going to call all the shots. She stared at him rebelliously.

His mouth quirked, his eyebrow lifted, and he reached into the top of her bathing suit, thrusting the handkerchief firmly between her breasts. "I think you have lovely pockets," he said.

His hand lingered a fraction of a second longer than it needed. He glanced down. The tug of the waves had pulled the neckline of her bathing suit down an inch or two. "Hmm," he said. "You're not one color all over. You're two-toned. I like that in a woman—two-toned pockets."

Another wave slapped at her face or she would have glared at him. Instead she was forced to squeeze her eyes shut. "Whitewater, you mouthy, mouthy beast, have I told you that I hate you?"

"Yes," he said, pulling her closer so that she wasn't swept away. "But only twice. Now, can you hang on to me without strangling me, or do you want me to hold you?"

"Both," Piper said, shutting her eyes more tightly against the assault of another wave.

"Your grandmother ought to be ashamed, scaring you of real water. The ocean is one of life's great joys."

Piper winced and choked as one of life's great joys hurled a wave of salty water into her mouth and temporarily blinded her, as well.

He sighed in exasperation as she shook her head and sputtered. "Look. I'm going to swim on my back. I'll tow you in a lifesaving hold. Don't fight me. If you have to hang on, lie kind of sideways and hold me around the waist. And trust me, dammit."

Piper gritted her teeth. She forced herself to disengage her arms from his neck, to lock them instead around the solid leanness of his waist. He draped one arm around her neck, and she could feel the pulse of his wrist beating hard and strong against the stammering vein in her throat.

He kicked off powerfully and she went rigid against him, feeling him propelling them both through the deepening water. When she opened her eyes, all she saw was sky and water rushing around them. She closed them again, pressing her face more firmly against the safety of his shoulder. He moved them deeper into the sea with more sureness and force than she'd imagined possible.

"Are you all right?" he asked once, his voice taut.

She clasped him more tightly. He had become the only solid thing in the world, the only safe thing. "No. I keep swallowing water."

"Ah," he said, as if it were a unique problem. "I know how to stop that."

She pressed her cheek harder against his straining bicep. "How?" she asked, already exhausted by the amount of water she'd consumed.

"Close your mouth," he said acidly.

She stiffened even more against him. "You know," she began, "I really do hate—" but the slap of sea water silenced her. She damned him mentally, but kept her mouth shut.

After what seemed like a major portion of eternity, David stopped and began treading water. "You do it, too," he ordered. "You can tread water, can't you?"

She nodded grimly. She looked apprehensively toward the shore. The beach was a thin white line, and the palm and coconut trees waved like dark and dainty feathers.

She forced herself to tread water and tried not to think how far her feet were from the ocean floor. "Okay," he said, moving behind her and slightly to her side. "I'm holding you, and you're fine, all right?"

She nodded with less conviction than before. His hands firmly clasped her waist. "Get the pearls," he said.

Taking a deep breath, she plunged her hand into her suit and took out the folded handkerchief.

"Now," he said, his breath warm against her ear and cheek. "Open it and count them."

Her hands shaking, she unfolded the corners of the soaked handkerchief. The eight pearls gleamed in its wet folds.

She stared down at them with more than the ocean's salt stinging her eyes. She had known them, loved their brightness, their irregularity, their mystery, from her childhood. She had seen them a thousand times. This was the last. She would never see them again.

She tried to turn her face to look into his eyes. She couldn't, not without struggling. She stared down at the pearls again. "I can't do it."

He held her more tightly. His lips were hot against her ear. "You have to."

She swallowed. "Does it say how? All at once? Or one at a time?"

He gave her an encouraging squeeze. "It doesn't say. Whatever you want."

Her first impulse was to drop them all at once. It would be the quickest and least painful way. She swallowed again, a hard unhappy lump in her throat. "I suppose one at a time. It seems more . . . respectful."

His arms slid around her more securely, holding her so that she didn't have to fear the water. "Then do it that way."

She stuffed the handkerchief back between her breasts. Then she held the pearls in her cupped hands and slowly opened her fingers. One pearl dropped from between them and disappeared silently into the sea, then another.

She watched, as if hypnotized into a sad trance, as they fell between her fingers until only one was left, the largest.

David said nothing for a moment. His jaw, hard and smooth, pressed against her cheek. "Go on," he whispered.

She thought of the olivine she had promised to save for Eloise. At least that much would be left. She opened her hands. The last pearl vanished into the water.

He turned her so that she faced him. She blinked hard and shook her head, her hands trailing emptily in the water. "I can't believe I did that," she said. She felt as if she were going to cry.

He merely looked at her. He reached and smoothed her bangs out of her eyes. "You did fine," he said at last.

He pulled her closer to him, and she felt his thighs tangling with her own as they both kicked to stay afloat. He bent his face nearer hers, and from the look in his eyes, for one dizzying moment Piper thought he was going to kiss her. Her heart made a crazed somersault and her lips parted slightly.

He smiled. Gently he took her jaw between his thumb and forefinger. "Remember what I said," he mocked. "It's safer to keep that pretty mouth shut."

She almost snapped it shut and looked away from him in hurt, but all she could see was the endless sweep of the ocean behind him, the sky growing grayer. "Take me back to shore," she ordered.

"Then come here," he muttered, sliding his arm around her neck again. "And don't hang on so tight this time. I've got this strange habit. I call it breathing."

In spite of his instructions, she clung to him more tightly than before. And in spite of her best efforts, she managed to swallow several more mouthfuls of the sea. When he finally drew her, coughing and gulping, onto the shore, Piper's knees felt too weak to support her. She stumbled in even the ankle-deep water.

She let him slide an arm around her waist and guide her, staggering, back to her beach towel. She threw herself face down on it and lay there a moment, panting.

He sat beside her, not even breathing hard. "Are you all right?" he asked again, although he seemed more amused than concerned.

"I never did like swimming," she said, profoundly grateful for the solidity of the sand beneath her. She stretched her length on it, as if assuring herself it was really there.

"That's ridiculous," he said, making her sit up. "Come on—we're running late. That took too long. How can you hate swimming?"

"Water's *eerie*," she replied with vehemence. "It's an alien world. And that much of it? It should scare anybody with any sense— Oh, forget it."

He smiled and reached for a towel. "Here," he said. "Dry your hair. I think one might be out of place."

Hastily she rubbed the towel over her hair and upper body. David, feigning politeness, helped her into her cover-up.

She took a hasty glance in the mirror of her compact. Her hair, though damp and salty, had fallen obediently back into place, and although her eyes were a bit reddened from salt water, she looked perfectly normal, not like a woman who had barely escaped death by drowning.

She snapped the compact shut, then gathered her belongings and stuffed them into the beach bag. She stood, her legs still shaky. David lay, lounging in the sand beside her, staring down the stretch of beach.

"If you're in such a hurry, come on," she told him. "What are you looking at?"

He frowned, the line appearing between his brows. "Nothing."

Putting on her sunglasses, Piper followed his gaze. About a hundred feet away, standing near the palms, was a small old woman, wearing a long red-and-white muumuu. Her skin was dark, her hair was white, and she held a red parasol over her head, as if for protection from sun or rain, although no sun beat down and no rain fell.

On a leash beside her was a small white dog with a shaggy coat and pointed ears. The woman had been facing David and Piper, her eyes hidden by the brim of a large white hat. As soon as Piper spied her, she and the dog turned toward a nearby stand of palms and disappeared among the trunks and shadows as easily as if they were shadows themselves.

David stood, his face more solemn and impassive than Piper had ever seen it. Suddenly, with a chill, she understood.

She looked up at him skeptically. "All right," she said. "An old lady in red with a little white dog. I know what you're thinking—Pele. Surely you don't believe all that superstition. That's a bunch of primitive rigmarole. You're a logical man. An educated one."

He was holding his yellow shirt, not bothering to put it on. He stared after the woman, although there was no longer any sign of her. He didn't smile. "Sometimes still . . . my heart is Sioux," he said.

She stared at him in perplexity. "What's that mean?" she asked. "Don't tell me you're going native on me. That's all I need."

That was the wrong thing to say, she thought in dismay. *That was a stupid thoughtless rude thing to say.*

She started to apologize but the cold look in his face stopped her. She knew an apology would be useless.

Without looking at her, he shrugged and put on his sunglasses, hiding his eyes. The line of his mouth had grown bitter. "I'm not 'going native.' I was born native." He shook his head. "Forget it. Don't worry. I don't think that way anymore."

She felt shut out, stricken. She regretted her words more than before. She had been exhausted and frustrated, and had spoken without thinking.

Once more she started to apologize, the words on the tip of her tongue. Instead she looked about.

The ocean foamed on one side, palm trees and exotic flowers nodded on the other. What a strange and enchanted place this was, Piper thought. Even the air, warm and fragrant, seemed to throb with mystery.

Did David feel it, too? Or did he even want to think about it? Eloise had said he was a man of reason, and his own brother had teased him about wanting everything to be logical. Was everything in the world a matter of logic or legality to him?

She glanced at his implacable profile, wondering uneasily if she would ever understand him. Or if he would understand her.

PIPER DID NOT LIKE the short flight over the ocean any better than she'd liked the long one. She was relieved when they stepped off the plane at the airport on the island of Hawaii.

Immediately she sensed this island differed greatly from Oahu. The small airport, partly open to the balmy air, dazzled the eye with its bright gardens. But its colorful flowers and glossy leaves seemed an oasis in the strangest wasteland she had ever seen.

Between the gardens of the airport and the distant glitter of the ocean stretched nothing but jagged dark rock, as irregular as rubble, as black as coal.

"Lava," David explained curtly when she asked. "Remember what Mary Lilola said. This is the newest island. The volcano's still at work."

Piper stood staring out at the stark scene while David went to rent a car. She inhaled the scents of the flowers, but her eyes were drawn to that bleak and hostile vista of black stone. She shuddered. If this was Pele's creation, it was forbidding.

The town of Kona, she was glad to find, was beautiful; it was smaller and less spoiled than Honolulu. Every spot of fertile earth seemed to burst with exotic flowers or trees.

"This place has two different faces," Piper said in wonder, as they checked into the hotel.

"What?" David said absently, taking the keys from the woman behind the desk.

"This island has two faces," Piper repeated, looking at the delicate flowers of an orchid tree in the lobby. "It's like the garden of Eden here. But between the airport and the ocean, a black desert."

David picked up her carry-on bag and threw the strap of his own over his shoulder. He seemed preoccupied. "This island has a thousand faces," he said between his teeth. "It's just a geological phenomenon. Come on. I'll drop you off and get our bags from the car. I'll take you for an early supper and then bring you back to the hotel. I've got things to do."

She looked up at him warily. "You have plans?"

He nodded without looking at her. "There's somebody I want to see. A woman."

Piper gave him a narrow sidelong glance as they entered one of the hotel's cluster of buildings. She didn't like being told he was abandoning her for better company. He had said he preferred Native American women. Did he know one here? "A woman? Another priestess?"

"A priestess? Hardly." He gave a short laugh she didn't understand.

In the lobby they passed an ornamental pool banked by brightly flowering plants. "Up these stairs," he said. "I'm afraid, once more, that your grandmother didn't pay for an ocean view. But I think your room may look out on part of the city."

Piper felt her heart growing flintier by the moment. David had steadfastly ignored her since their conversation on the beach, and now he was insulting her grandmother again. If he resented Piper's remarks about going native, at least he could take into consideration what he had put her through that morning. Instead he'd spent the flight from Oahu to Hawaii reading his damnable and everlasting book.

"How dare you complain about not having an ocean view?" she asked with asperity. "After my grandmother's paid for everything, and you're just along...freeloading?"

They gained the fourth floor and he walked down the hall so fast she practically had to run to keep up. He didn't stop until he reached the farthest room.

He didn't bother to look at her. "Carting you all over these islands is no vacation." He thrust one of the keys into the lock, twisted it and swung open the door.

"There," he said, putting down her carryon. "I'll be back with your tastefully matched bags of tastefully matched clothing. And I'm not worried about my room's not having a view. I was only thinking of you. It'd be nice, since you've come so far. It might broaden your personal horizons."

"That's absolutely unfair," she retorted. "My personal horizons are as broad as anybody's."

He only smiled, unlocked his own room, and stepped inside. His lock clicked shut as if taunting her.

She swore at him under her breath, one vivid word about the legality of his ancestry. Squaring her shoulders, she entered her own room.

It was small, serviceable and devoid of any hint of luxury. David had been right. If she stepped to one of its windows, she could just see a few of the green-lined streets of Kona. From her other window, however, she looked down into a parking lot.

If Eloise was going to send her three thousand miles, Piper thought grumpily, the least she could have done was reserve her a room with a better view than a parking lot.

She turned from the window angrily, cursing David Whitewater for planting such an idea in her mind. Eloise would say that scenery is free. Why should anyone pay to look at it? If Piper wanted to see it, she had two perfectly good legs to carry her outside to do so.

She sat on the edge of the bed and picked up the telephone receiver and tried to call her grandmother again. It was three o'clock in Hawaii, therefore seven in Nebraska. Eloise would almost certainly be home.

But the phone rang, unanswered. Nobody answered at Harold's house, either. Piper felt a tiny surge of panic. Was something wrong? Had the baby come early or had there been some other unforeseen event? Should she take a chance and phone Jeannie? What was happening? Where were they all? Where was Eloise?

THAT EVENING Piper sat across from David at an ocean-front table at a downtown restaurant. The room was open to the evening breeze, and if she looked over the rail, she could see the surf crashing against the rocks almost directly beneath her.

"So what does it feel like?" David asked during his dessert. "To throw away a couple of thousand dollars worth of pearls?"

She put her hand to her forehead in a gesture of disgust. She was uneasy because she still hadn't been able to reach Eloise. "Worse than you'll ever know. I don't want to talk about it."

She'd been able to eat little. She took another sip of wine, her second glass.

"I don't know why you ever agreed to this," he said, "if it makes you feel this bad."

She toyed with a bread stick, broke it in half and set it on her plate, untasted. "I didn't have any choice. In the first place, according to this 'ritual,' a member of my family is *supposed* to do it."

He shook his head, his mouth set dubiously. "Responsibilities can be delegated. Compromises can be made."

"Really? Nobody told us," Piper said sarcastically, keeping her hand over her eyes.

She didn't want to look at him. He wore a peacock-blue knit shirt that hugged his muscles and matched his eyes. He looked so handsome in it, it irritated her in the extreme. She wished he had spiky tufts of hair springing out of his ears and crooked green fangs.

"In the second place," she said, "I owe it to my grandmother. I know you don't like her, but she's done everything for me. Everything. This is the least I can do for her."

"Why not?" he asked with cheerful insolence. "You'll end up with everything. Except, of course, the necklace."

"Listen," Piper said, too frustrated to wrestle down her resentment, "I'm *not* my grandmother's only heir. I'll end up with exactly the same share as everybody else: my aunt, my uncle, my brother, my cousins. And we *don't,* for your information, split up 'everything.' Most of her money and all of her art collection go to the museum. So stop acting as if I'm going to inherit half of North America, all right?"

The look he shot her was skeptical. "What about her other property? The jewelry stores?"

Piper picked up the mutilated bread stick and broke it into fours. "Forty-nine percent of the stock goes to the museum to maintain the wing they'll build in her name," she recited. She had known the statistics since childhood.

"Thirty percent goes into trust funds and allowances for the relatives. Twenty percent goes to the Scottish Benevolent Society. I'll own a whopping five percent. I'll get a small inheritance when she...when she dies. My share of store profits goes into a trust fund. Which I get when I'm fifty. Not that any of this is your business. I'd just like to set the record straight. I'm not exactly heiress material."

The familiar frown line manifested itself between his eyebrows. He put his elbows on the table and made a tent of his fingers. "Wait a minute," he said, his mouth more cynical than ever. "She's leaving you none of the art collection, which is probably the most valuable thing she owns."

"It's her greatest joy," Piper said with feeling. "She doesn't want it split up."

"So you and each of your relatives get only five percent of the jewelry-store holdings?" He did a series of mental calculations. "She's not treating you with any particular generosity. Sounds like a woman more interested in vanity than family."

"That's unfair," Piper retorted. "It's her money. She married my grandfather when he had only one jewelry store. When he died, she built it, single-handedly, into the chain it's become. She doesn't believe in . . . in weakening us by promising we'll always have easy money. And she's never stooped to trying to buy our affection. She's never promised anybody anything extra or cut anybody off. Her plan has always been to leave most of her estate to the museum, and that's her right."

"Let me get this straight," David said. "She made the money, so if she wants to spend it on her own glory, it's all right with you."

"It's *hers*," Piper insisted. "If she wants to make a gift of it to the public, more power to her."

"But she's training you to manage the stores some day. What do you get out of that?"

"A salary from the estate," she said impatiently. "Exactly what anybody else would get in my place."

"That's all?" he asked in disbelief. "My God, she hasn't found a way to take it with her, but she's come close. Why bother being her toady? Why not strike out on your own?"

"I can't," she said, raising her chin. "When she's gone, it's *my* responsibility. Not just the stores—the family. Somebody's got to take care of them."

David's upper lip curled. "Why? Can't they take care of themselves?"

Piper took a deep breath, sensing she'd already said too much. "No," she said, thinking of Jeannie and her poor twins. "As a matter of fact, they can't. But that's all right, because *I* can. And my grandmother's always known it and believed in me and trusted me to do it. And I'm proud she does."

"So Grandma dies and is enshrined forever by the art museum. You draw a salary, do the work and worrying for the rest of the family and, if you're a good little draft horse, you'll be rewarded when you're fifty."

"Oh, get that superior smirk off your face," she told him, breaking the bread stick into tiny fragments. "You make me sound like a fool. My grandmother has trained me for an extremely important position."

"And what's wrong with the rest of the family? What do they do while you fight to hold everything together?"

Piper took a long sip of her wine and stared down at the surf. She refused to tell him more. They were none of his concern—Jeannie's tragedy, her fears and crying fits, the welfare of the twins, Harold's flightiness, MacDowell's defection.

"I asked you a question," David said. "Why do you have to take care of everybody? Why can't they take care of themselves?"

She steeled herself to meet his eyes and did it as coolly as Eloise herself might have done. "A strange question from a man who makes a career of watching out for other people's interests. Why don't you let your precious Native Americans fend for themselves? Or can't they take care of themselves, either?"

He sat up straighter. Icy fire flashed deep in his eyes. "My God," he said out of the corner of his mouth. "You're her blood, all right. A real street fighter. Do you know how vicious that question is?"

The waiter appeared and asked her if she wanted more wine. She shook her head to indicate she did not; the two glasses she'd already had were making her head throb.

"It wasn't any more vicious than the things you're asking me," she countered, her own eyes flashing. "My family needs help. You seem to think your people do. What's the difference?"

"The difference is," he drawled with exaggerated deliberation, "that your family hasn't been oppressed for three hundred years. The difference is that your grandmother is a ruthless conniving rich old lady. I know she didn't mind ripping off the Navahos. I did think she might have second thoughts about ripping off her own family."

"My grandmother never tried to cheat the Navahos."

"So she keeps saying. A court said otherwise. Did it ever occur to you, Piper, that your precious grandmother might be as guilty as hell?"

"She wasn't," Piper protested. "She's tough, but she's honest. I don't know why her records were faulty—it was something about her supplier wanting cash. He's the one who lied and cheated, not her. She's a wonderful woman. And she's taken wonderful care of her family. Wonderful."

"Right," he said disdainfully. "Such good care that they can't take care of themselves. You're supposed to spend the rest of your life baby-sitting. They sound like a bunch—" He cut himself off. He gave her a challenging glance but said no more.

David stood, throwing down the money for the waiter's tip. "Let's get out of here," he growled. "I've got other things to do."

Like seeing your woman? Piper thought bitterly, but she said nothing. She was angry, extremely angry, but she managed to rein in her emotions while he paid the bill and they left the restaurant.

"I'll walk you back to the hotel," he said, taking her arm when they reached the foot of the restaurant steps. They stood in the shadow of a huge banyan tree. "I'm sorry I was critical of your family. Forget it."

Piper wasn't about to forget and she refused to budge. She jerked her arm away and glared at him. His face was stony and unreadable in the half-light.

"What's so great about *your* family, Whitewater?" she asked, the blood pounding in her temples. "Where's the fortune they built? The museum they'll endow? The business they'll pass on? You make fun of my family's 'noble blood.' What's so wonderful about yours?"

He took a step toward her. He put his hands on her upper arms. Almost roughly he drew her more deeply into the shadows of the banyan.

He bent his face close to hers, speaking through clenched teeth. "They don't have any fortune. They can't endow anything. They owned damned little. And by your standards, my blood probably isn't even respectable. Your grandmother made that abundantly clear to me when she handed over the necklace. Abundantly."

It wasn't the first time his intensity had taken her aback, but she refused to be intimidated. She stood her ground, breathing hard. "It still comes down to the same thing—I'm taking care of mine," she said, "and you're taking care of yours. But you act as if your cause is high and mighty. But it comes down to the same thing as for me—family."

"No," he said, his hands tightening, and his voice bitter. "I don't have much family. And what's left takes care of itself."

"Really?" she taunted. "Who—besides you and your brother? And he's much more civil than you are, by the way."

"Blood relatives?" His hands tightened on her arms until his grip was almost painful. "Do you really want to know? An aunt. A cousin. All the rest I ever knew are dead. All of them. My grandfather, two uncles. Two cousins. Our mother. Our father—we think. We're not sure what happened to him.''

He shook her slightly to make her listen. ''But I saw what killed the others, and I can tell you—poverty, disease and despair. Do you really want details? Have you really got the guts to listen? To what I've seen happen—not just to a family—but a people?''

She tried to twist from his grasp, but she couldn't escape; he was far too strong, and his emotion was running too high and too hot. ''Stop it,'' she said.

''No,'' he countered. ''I'll never stop. Not until I get justice. I won't quit. Not until I've evened the odds for my people. I'll fight. I've learned to think like a white man, and I've learned to use his weapons—the laws and the courts— and I use them with all the force I've got.''

''You're not using any weapon but strength,'' she told him contemptuously. ''This has nothing to do with the law, not this.'' She looked down in anger at the lean brown hands gripping her arms.

''Because your family wants to be above the law,'' he almost hissed. ''You make me wish it were the old days. Handling you would be pure and simple.''

''Why?'' she asked recklessly. ''What would you do? Something primitive? Set the stockade on fire?''

He drew her a fraction of an inch nearer. ''Woman,'' he said, ''there'd be flames like you never imagined.''

Almost before she knew it, he was kissing her. Her world turned to darkness and caught fire.

CHAPTER SIX

DAVID DREW BACK from her abruptly. His hands returned to her shoulders, more gently than before, but still holding her prisoner. His breath came raggedly, and his dark forelock had fallen across his brow.

Hurriedly, shakily, Piper pulled her defenses together. She tossed her head and set her mouth. "What was that, Mr. Whitewater? Your learned legal opinion?—or a warning that you're on the warpath and taking no prisoners?"

"I think it was a warning, all right," he agreed, the set of his jaw grim. "That we should keep our distance. I didn't mean for that to happen."

His voice sounded cold with control, but still he didn't release her. He gripped her shoulders more tightly and drew her a fraction of an inch nearer.

Although the blood pounded in her cheeks, and her lips stung from his kiss, she kept her face as impassive as his. "Let me go. I'll walk back by myself, thank you."

"No," he said. "You're not going alone. I'm supposed to watch out for you. So let me tell you something—this is an island of fire. And fire is not a force to play with."

Her expression stiffened with anger. "Playing with fire? Are you implying I *asked* for that? Don't you dare. I was arguing with you, trying to use . . . to use logic and reason, and the next thing I know you . . . you've *ambushed* me."

"You wouldn't know a logical argument if it fell in your lap. And you don't know when you've pushed a man too damn far. And furthermore . . ."

He paused, staring down at her. Even in the shadows she could see the muscle twitch in his cheek, playing near the spot his dimple showed in happier times.

She stood as straight and prim as an old-fashioned schoolmarm. "Furthermore?" she said, sounding more flippant than she felt.

"Furthermore," he said at last, "you don't know how you look in the moonlight and shadows."

His words, his look, made a dizzying sensation dance along her nerves.

"Or maybe you do," he said with a weary sigh. He let her go, holding his hands out briefly from his sides in a gesture that said he was tired of the situation.

"My brother warned me about this," he muttered with ill humor. He turned toward the hotel and started walking. He gave her a curt nod to signal her to come along.

She hesitated a moment, then caught up with him. "Your brother warned you about what?" she demanded. She didn't think she'd made a bad impression on Aaron Whitewater. She didn't think she'd made any impression at all.

They walked past an empty stretch of shore where the surf pounded the black rock. "All this," he said, nodding to indicate the ocean and palm trees. "Getting mixed up with women and islands and volcanoes. Aaron said to watch out. It's a *witkokaga* in our family. But I'm not superstitious. I've never believed any of it." He swore.

"*Witko*-what?" Piper asked, puzzled. "Is that Hawaiian?"

"It's Sioux. It means a crazy-making spirit. Crazy."

She didn't understand, and she could tell from the shuttered look on his face that asking him would do no good. Spirits again, she thought with foreboding.

THE NEXT MORNING Piper tried to call Eloise at both private numbers. There was still no answer. Harold's number was busy. She was about to break down and call one of the jewelry-store managers when David knocked at the door, ready to take the black pearls from the necklace.

She gave up her attempt to reach Eloise and watched, half-sick as he pried the pearls free and wrapped them in his handkerchief. She felt stricken, as if it were part of her childhood, her life, he was destroying.

As they drove toward the green sand beach, she tried not to think of her grandmother's inexplicable silence or the mutilated necklace. She was fortunate, for the island of Hawaii had witchery to even soothe thoughts as troubling as hers.

"This place is not real," Piper said as they wound along the road from Kona in their rented silver Ford compact. "This land is not *possible*. I'm hallucinating. It can't change so completely every five miles."

David gave her a cool sidelong look. He had remained uncommunicative during most of the meandering trip. "You're not hallucinating. It changes."

Piper settled against the seat, staring out. When they had left Kona, vegetation flourished in tropical profusion on every side of them: ginger and spider lilies, mango and plumeria trees, ferns and palms.

Then before she knew it, they were ascending a stark mountain of lava as black as onyx and completely bare of plant life. As the car took a turn, the world became green again and they passed through orchards of macadamia-nut trees with their delicate leaves.

Another turn brought them to a second desert of black lava, only one not so desolate as the first. On this one strange plants bloomed in tufts.

Another crook in the road and Piper looked out over meadows and flower farms. Everything was blossoming and tame. Only five miles farther brought rough fields of rusty red, thick with strange gasses and shrubs. This gave way to ranch land that looked as Western as Wyoming.

Somewhere in the eerie journey, Piper remembered, there had also been deep green gorges studded with the bright orange of the African tulip trees, and long waterfalls that plunged in a crystal rush.

"David, this is the strangest place I've ever seen," she said. An exotic pheasant burst up from the underbrush and whirred across the road, flying low.

"I told you. This island has a thousand faces."

"I always thought Hawaii was a big rain forest surrounded by beaches."

"Another illusion shattered," he said tonelessly.

She gave him a disapproving glance, which he, as usual, ignored. "I'm glad the illusion's shattered," she protested. "I'm interested. I want to understand, that's all. Is it because of the volcano?"

"Bingo," he said, then lapsed into silence.

"David!"

"Excuse me?" he said, turning and lifting his eyebrow in question. "Am I wearing a tour guide's hat? No, I don't think so." He turned his attention back to the road.

"David!" she repeated furiously. She had tried to be civil all morning and afternoon. He had not. Her patience snapped. She wished the volcano were nearby so that she could push him into it.

"To your left," he said in a mock tour-guide voice she immediately hated, "is lava with stuff growing out of it. To your right is lava without stuff growing out of it. That, more or less, is what happens. This island was built from lava flows, old and new. Things either grow out of it, or they don't."

Piper watched unhappily as the lava was transformed mysteriously into pasture land again. "Have I told you lately that I hate you?"

"No. This is the first time today. Ah. This is our turn. South Cape's where we want to go."

"I bought a postcard," she said moodily as they passed more pastureland. "On the back it said there were twenty-two possible climates in the world, and this island had twenty-one of them. I didn't believe it. Now I do."

The road began to snake downward. David shrugged. "The highest mountain on this island has snow. Mark Twain wrote about standing there, eating a snowball and looking down at the tropical palms on the coast. He called it 'all the earth's zones—concentrated.' He said almost every climate existed on that stretch, between the mountaintop and the coast. Maybe ten miles as the crow flies."

It didn't seem possible, Piper thought, yet she had seen it with her own eyes. No wonder people believed in Pele. This island was so varied, so full of contrasts, it was like a miniature of the wealth of creation itself.

The car bounced down the rutted road. A stony black shore lay at the road's end, and beyond it stretched the ocean, wild and foaming as the waves rolled in. Black chunks of lava edged the sea like a tumble of great cinders. Farther from the sea, the earth was rust-colored and grassed in a wild pale green.

Piper counted a dozen fishing and pleasure boats parked on boat trailers. The waves pounding in were bright blue, an aqua blue laced with snowy foam. The place was eerily deserted. The only sounds were the thunder of the waves and the echo of the wind.

David got out of the car and came around, opening her door. "From here we walk."

"Walk?" Piper asked, looking at the rugged landscape. Green hills, studded with rough black boulders, stretched out behind them. It was both beautiful and desolate.

"How far?" she asked, getting out. Immediately the wind tugged at her white slacks, her pink cotton sweater. Its force tossed her hair, slapped her face. The air was warm and salty, and the waves roared against the shore in a turquoise cavalcade.

David frowned as he looked down the lava-strewn coast. "The guidebook says two miles. A guy at the hotel said one. Aaron's never been here, but he estimated three. I'd trust Aaron."

He turned to her, frowning harder as he looked at her skimpy white sandals. "Didn't you bring any other shoes? I told you to wear walking shoes."

"These *are* walking shoes," she said, raising her voice to be heard over the wind. Her sweater and slacks flapped in its relentless force.

He raised a dubious eyebrow. "We'll see." He started down a red dirt road that looked more like a cow path than footway for humans. Piper squared her shoulders, lowered her sunglasses against the wind's sting and followed. On either side of them, the stunted grasses waved wildly.

David wore low-rise faded jeans, running shoes and a wine-colored knit shirt that the harsh wind sculpted against his body. Piper hurried to catch up, dodging a large rut filled with red mud. It was like walking through a strange primeval meadow, where the wind had blown from the beginning of time and would blow until the end.

"Where are we? South Cape?" she asked. "There's nothing here." And there was nothing except the elements: crashing blue ocean, black stone, ancient green mountains and brilliant sunlight. And the ceaseless blast of the coursing air. They might have been the only two human beings alive.

"The beach is here—somewhere," he said, striding along. The gusts made his hair a black tangle against the blue sky. "This is the southernmost point of the United States. You can't go any farther south and still be in America. This is it."

Piper looked around once more, taking in the emerald folds of the hills, the ebony shore, the pure blue aquamarine of the waves. She had never thought of Hawaii having such isolated spots, only crowded beaches and busy harbors.

She felt odd in such a lonely exotic place, almost as if they had fallen backward in time. The wind pushed at them so hard that for a moment she was almost convinced it was trying to keep them out of some sacred place.

She bent her head and kept going. "Why do you think we're supposed to get rid of the black pearls here? Why a green sand beach?" she asked.

"Ask your Portuguese wizard," David said. They both had to talk loudly to make themselves heard. He took her arm to help her make her way around a particularly deep rut.

"He's not *my* wizard," Piper protested, pulling away from his touch. Any contact with him sent currents of excitement streaming through her that were as powerful as the wind, and she hated her response. "I think he was a scheming old fraud."

"Well, he must have been a damn good scheming old fraud, because two hundred years later he's got you dancing to the tune he played."

"Do you always have to rub salt in the wound? You're dancing the same dance," she said. She stopped to get her breath, and ran the back of her hand across her forehead. She already felt windburned and feverish. "Look," she said, staring at the ground. "Is that green sand?"

She pointed to a few grains of sand lying in a furrow of the muddy path. Against the red dirt, they seemed almost green—a dull olive color.

"I don't know," was all he said.

"You're very closemouthed today," Piper challenged. "What's the matter? Did you stay out late last night? I never heard you come in."

"I didn't come in. Until this morning."

She glanced up. His profile was unreadable, his eyes fixed on some distant point, his hair tossed by the unceasing wind. He looked so lean and handsome against the green rolling hills that Piper's heart gave a painful and unwanted lurch.

"Then I guess you found your lady-friend," she said, rather tartly. "I thought you'd taken a vow of chastity for this trip. How interesting—wasn't that part of the ritual?"

He gave her a brief look, his eyes snapping blue sparks. "I didn't find her. Maybe when we come back."

Piper was hot, tired and irritable. Her shoes pinched and the wind punished her face. She was in no mood to deal with David's cryptic and unfriendly responses. "Then what were you doing out all night?"

He tossed her another eloquent glance. "I was thinking, all right? I sat by the sea and I thought."

"All night long?" Her voice was dubious.

"Yes," he said between clenched teeth. "All night long."

"And just what," she asked, trying to smooth her hair, "does one spend all night thinking about? How much fun it is to torture my grandmother?"

"I have better things to think about than your grandmother, the felon."

"Of course. How foolish of me. Such as?"

"Such as *my* family," he said with such intensity she was taken aback. "I was thinking about my family, all right?"

They walked on in silence. Piper looked about. The scene filled her with perplexity: the strange hills studded with black lava, the harsh black shore, the tender blue of the waves and, above all, the solitude. She and David might have been walking on an alien planet.

She thought she had seen lines of strain about his eyes when he had come into her room to cut the black pearls from the necklace. But she had pushed it from her mind; she was still angry with him for his actions of the night before. Besides, he was mutilating the necklace even more. The black pearls, although small and irregular, were to Piper the most romantic part of the necklace. She had hated him as he snipped the silver chain that held them, then pried them from their settings.

Now, however, in this eerie and windswept wild, she regretted the anger that had flared between them. It seemed petty, insignificant. They walked on, saying nothing, while the wind wailed around them, louder than the sea.

"Look," she said at last. "I'm sorry about last night. I didn't mean to insult your family. I spoke in anger."

He didn't look at her. He kept his attention focused on some distant thing she could not see. "It's all right," he finally answered. "I said some things I shouldn't have myself. And did a few." A vein leapt in his temple, then stilled.

"Well," she said, trying to heal the breach, "you and my grandmother have been enemies. You clashed in court. It's natural you don't like her. But I love her, the same way you love your family."

He shook his head. "Love," he said bitterly.

"I mean," she offered, feeling awkward, "you and your brother are obviously close."

He nodded ironically. "Close. I guess you might say that."

Her mouth was dry, her face burned from the assault of the wind, her legs throbbed with tiredness, and once more David was driving her to new reaches of frustration.

"I guess," she said, "I'm trying to ask you about them. About your family." She tried, again unsuccessfully, to smooth her hair.

He stayed silent a long moment. Then he cast her a skeptical glance, as if he didn't believe her.

"No," she said. "Really. I'd like to know."

She thought she saw the ghostly smile hovering at the corner of his mouth. "Enough to answer a few questions about your own?"

Piper shrugged philosophically. "It's a long walk. Why not?"

"Okay. What about your mother and father?"

Her face grew solemn. "My father left us. My mother got sick and he wasn't able to deal with it."

"Ever hear from him?"

Piper bit her lip. "No. I don't mind. I never knew him that well."

"And your mother?"

She bit her lip harder. "Dead. When I was ten."

"Who else? Besides your grandmother and your aunt?"

"Two cousins. A brother and sister-in-law. An uncle. But he went away."

"Why?"

"Grandmother says he was seduced by late-blooming hippiedom. He wanted to do his own thing."

David's mouth took on a sardonic crook she didn't like.

"She expected MacDowell to help with all her responsibilities, but he wouldn't." Piper groped for words. "He was...selfish."

"Why?" David demanded. "Because he wanted his own life?"

Piper gritted her teeth. "He *was* selfish. He wanted the lion's share of the business, and he didn't want her to give away the art collection. She wouldn't knuckle under to him. I told you, she'd never buy anybody's loyalty or affection. She wouldn't stoop to that. She wouldn't give him any more. But she wouldn't give him any less. She's still leaving him the same as everybody else." She saw the mocking light in his eyes. "Don't laugh," she ordered with spirit.

"Who's laughing? Money's a serious subject."

"I saw your mouth twitch."

"It was thirst. I should have listened to Aaron. He said to bring water. I didn't think we'd need it for six measly miles."

"So what about you?" she challenged. "It's your turn."

"What about me?"

"What about your mother and father?"

His face became less readable than ever. "He was Sioux. She was white—Danish mostly. They didn't get along. She left. He was in the navy and got sent to Japan. My grandfather took Aaron and me. Back to the reservation."

"Your parents—you said they're dead?"

He nodded laconically, as if he were talking about people unrelated to him. "I heard she died a few years ago. She didn't want to see us. We were a mistake she wanted to forget. My father died in Japan. We don't know how exactly."

His face was impassive but bitterness resonated in his tone. She realized her childhood had probably been one of security and luxury compared to his.

"So your grandfather raised you?"

His face went no softer at the memory. "Till I was thirteen. Then he died. And Aaron and my aunt—Cora—made me go off to private school. Probably took every spare dime they had. That didn't work, so they tried military school. God, I hated it."

There was no mistaking the degree of passion in his voice or the look of abhorrence that crossed his face.

She studied him furtively, the sudden tension in his face, the slightly dangerous swing his shoulders had taken on.

"I'm sorry," she said.

"Probably saved my life," he said, shaking his head. "They didn't have much choice. I was wild. Very wild. The old man couldn't handle me at all by the end. I was drinking, helling around..." He shrugged and went silent.

"Is that why you hardly ever drink now?"

"That's why. Drinking killed two of my uncles. *Minne sheetska,* my grandfather used to say. The bad water. Whiskey. Who needs it? Not me."

"And the rest of your family?"

"Gone," he said, his face grim.

"Only you and Aaron? And your aunt?"

For the first time he smiled. "One cousin. Nighthorse."

"Nighthorse?" Piper asked.

"Hey, I didn't laugh at your hippie uncle. Don't make fun of my cousin Nighthorse."

"I've just never heard of anybody named Nighthorse."

"His full name is Bradford Nighthorse Whitewater. Sportswriters made the Nighthorse part permanent."

"He's an athlete?"

"That's what saved him."

"Saved him?"

He stopped smiling. "Look. The Sioux stood up to the U.S. government. At Little Big Horn, we gave the military the worst beating of its history. So it decided to crush us. The reservation system nearly crushed us, too. It isn't easy to survive that." He swore again at the memory.

"What saved you?"

He glanced up at the sky. "Boxing. And debate, if you can believe it. I kept getting into trouble at military school. Aaron came to talk to the commander. Then he stalked into my room and threw me against the wall—hard. He said, 'Dave, you blankety-blank, you think you're tougher than everybody? You think you're smarter? You want to fight? Do it in a ring. You want to argue? Do it in a classroom. Or else.' And then he threw me against the wall again."

Piper's eyes widened. Nobody had ever struck her in her life.

He studied the expression on her face. "Hey. I asked for it."

She regarded him warily. "What happened?"

"There was only one thing to do."

"What?"

"Prove I *was* tougher and smarter than everybody."

He gave her a lazy mischievous grin, and for a moment she glimpsed the devil he must have been. "And I did," he said. "Nobody ever beat me—in the ring or at debate."

Piper didn't doubt it. He looked like a bronze god to her, tall and burnished, the sunlight dancing in his black hair.

She thought perhaps she understood him better now: a man who had known grinding poverty and injured pride, an outsider fighting the establishment on the behalf of other outsiders.

"Is that how to handle you then?" she asked, forcing lightness into her voice. "Just throw you against the wall from time to time?"

"Maybe. But Aaron's the only one who could ever do that."

Piper didn't doubt it. Nobody would ever control David—except David himself.

Her head began to ache dully. She ran the back of her hand across her forehead again. "It's so hot. This wind—doesn't it ever stop?"

"It must be the famous Kona Wind."

She swallowed dryly, suddenly frightened by what they were going to have to do. She looked out at the blue tossing waves with troubled eyes.

"The water's so rough," she said, shaking her head. "How can we ever get out there to drop the pearls?"

The farther they went, the more rugged the coastline grew. Jagged black rocks jutted into the sea and waves flumed up against them like geysers. The water in Honolulu had been placid compared to this hurling sea.

He stopped for a moment and she stopped with him, glad to rest. His gaze narrowed as he watched the waves crash against the ragged black rocks. "Don't worry," he said at last. He looked down at her and once more she was jarred by the color of his eyes. They were as blue as the wild waves.

"I'll have you," he said, his voice low.

I'll be fine, she thought, her heart beating almost as hard as the crashing surf. *You'll have me.*

He stared into her eyes. He nodded.

CHAPTER SEVEN

PIPER'S FEET HURT and her sandals were covered with red mud. Her mouth was parched, her lungs stinging from the ceaseless wind.

Thick beds of vegetation now edged the path, strange low-lying plants with fat waxy leaves and yellow flowers. They looked so soft and cool she wanted to sink into them and rest.

The surf boomed ominously against the black shore, and more and more she wondered how she and David would keep from being beaten to pieces against the lava when they entered the ocean. All of yesterday's fears returned stronger than before. Physically she was becoming too tired to put up even a feeble fight against the sea.

Then she glimpsed a patch of flat dull greenness ahead, and hope swelled in her heart.

"Look," she cried, pointing. "That's it—the green sand beach. Thank God. I don't think I could go any farther."

"Sorry," he said as they approached. It was, indeed, a tiny stretch of smooth green sand edged by lava and littered with white driftwood. "I don't think this is it."

"It has to be," Piper said. "How many green sand beaches can there be?"

"This is only two miles." He shook his head. "I don't think you can really call it a beach. Aaron said another mile. We've only gone two."

"*Only* two?" she objected. "How far is three?"

He pointed at a black cliff that seemed incredibly far off.

"That," he said, "is three. And I see more green up there. That must be the real beach."

Piper dropped wearily onto a bleached chunk of driftwood. She was hot, windburned and sure her feet were blistered. "No." She said the word firmly. "No farther. If I'm going to be beaten to death by waves, I'm not going to hike another mile to do it. This is sand, it's green, and it's going to have to do."

She picked up a handful of the sun-warmed grains and let them run soothingly through her fingers. They gleamed like bits of glass.

David stood, his thumbs hooked in the front pockets of his jeans, staring down at her. She sat, breathing hard. She licked her lips, which felt cracked and dry.

"All right," he muttered. "It's green and it's sand. Fair enough. You're actually starting to look a little ragged around the edges."

She shook her head, which pounded from the heat. She picked up another handful of sand. "Why is it like this? It really is green. I feel like I'm on another planet."

He watched her, as if measuring exactly how much strength she had left. "For the same reason the olivine in the necklace is green. It's something that can happen when hot lava hits the sea. Don't get any in your shoes. Madame Pele doesn't like it when people carry off her property."

Piper put her elbows on her knees and bent her head, resting it in her hands. "Let her keep her sand. And please don't tell me you believe that sort of nonsense—cursed for sand in my shoes? *Please.*"

There was a beat of silence. "I don't believe in her. But if I did, I'd give her credit for doing nice work."

She raised her head and tried to take in the improbable scene: green sand, blue sky, bluer sea, alien yet beautiful yellow flowers. "Yes," she said softly. "She does do lovely work. Lovely."

She picked up another handful of green sand and thought of the olivine. For the first time, the idea of keeping any of it gave her a guilty twinge. But she had promised Eloise. And as Eloise had said, who could begrudge her such a small souvenir?

"Are you ready?" he asked, and distracted her by drawing off his shirt. "We might as well get it over with. Maybe you'll feel better after you get in the water."

"I seriously doubt that," she said, remembering the day before. But she sighed and pulled off her pink sweater. She wore a pale blue one-piece tank suit beneath. She stood, kicked off her sandals, undid her slacks and stepped out of them.

The wind rushed around her nearly naked body, making it tingle, and the sand was hot beneath her bare feet. She took off her sunglasses and set them carefully beside her beach bag. Without her tinted lenses, the ocean looked even more supernaturally blue.

David stepped out of his jeans. He wore black trunks with a stripe down each side, and as she looked at the restless sea behind him, she was suddenly glad that he seemed all long lean muscle. The breadth of his shoulders reassured her, as did the biceps that glistened in the sunlight. The tightly packed sinews of his thighs rippled when he took a step toward her, and the muscles of his chest played when he reached his hand to her.

"What—?" she asked.

He drew her to him. "I'll carry you," he said. "Your feet won't be able to take the lava."

Piper stiffened slightly, pulses thudding even harder as his hand tightened around hers. "What do you do? Walk on fire in your spare time? I can walk on it as well as you."

"I usually run ten miles a day. I'm tough. You can't even *walk* two miles without wimping out. Come to Papa."

He stooped slightly, winding one arm beneath her bare legs. His other looped beneath her arm and went around her waist. Effortlessly he hoisted her into the air, her feet kicking in feeble protest.

"Don't wiggle," he warned, frowning. "This is going to be hard enough. Behave."

His chest was like a hard wall of stone, one warmed by the sun, and his arms wrapped her so securely her body could barely move. Where her bare flesh touched his, she seemed to burn.

He carried her across the small patch of green sand, then, more slowly, down the black shore, stepping carefully among the jumbled stones. She looked down and saw lava as edged and razor sharp as chunks of slag glass.

The ocean boomed more loudly in her ears, and when she felt the first hints of spray on her body, it chilled her in spite of the heat.

She tightened her arms around his neck. Suddenly she no longer wanted to see. The lava looked too cruel, the waves too strong; she could imagine the killing power of the surf hurling her against the stone. A person could be battered unconscious and then to death.

Tensing in his arms, she fought the desire to lay her face against his neck and hide her eyes.

"Have you got the pearls?" he asked. His lips were close to her ear, making it tickle.

She nodded, closing her eyes. The pearls lay, wrapped in his handkerchief, between her breasts as before.

He moved more slowly, more deliberately now, for the lava was wet, slick with sea water. The waves crashed so loudly she could not even hear the wind that whipped at them.

She sensed he was stepping closer still to the water. "Whitewater," she said miserably, "I don't like this."

"Hold me tighter," he ordered. She did. She stopped fighting the urge to bury her face against his shoulder. It was warm and solid against her cheek, and she wished she could burrow inside him and live for the next few minutes entirely protected by his muscle.

"Tighter still," he said. She squeezed against him as hard as she could.

"I really don't like it," she said, and hated herself for admitting it.

"I'm not crazy about it myself," he said. "That water's choppy. Look, just pretend we're going surfing. I'll swim out on top of the water. I'll need both arms. You hang on to my neck. Watch when you breathe. Don't keep taking a mouthful of water the way you did yesterday. Understand?"

She nodded, her teeth clenched. She realized she was shaking all over and again she hated herself. "Now," he said, and she felt him nearing the pounding surf. "Just trust me. Who's the toughest guy you know?"

She swallowed. "You are," she said, pressing harder against his shoulder.

"And the smartest?"

"You are," she said, unshed tears of fear burning her eyes.

"So," he said, his voice remarkably cheerful, "what have you got to worry about? Breathe deep. Hang on..."

Piper obeyed. Suddenly she was in the center of a roiling spinning swirl of water. She clung to David's neck so tightly she wondered how he could breathe, but somehow, in spite of her grip and the power of the incoming waves, he propelled them outward.

Terror of the water shook through her in convulsive shudders and her throat already burned from inhaling spray. She had the claustrophobic feeling of being trapped between the waves, and she wanted to struggle, but knew it could be dangerous, even fatal. She could only hang on, hating the taste of seawater in her mouth, hating the way it bit at her eyes.

When they were in a calm spot, her head above water, her face touched by blessed air, she gasped wildly.

"Breathe!" David ordered. "Again. Deep breath."

She obeyed and then they were plunged under a hellish surge of water again. He was bearing her into the waves more deeply, more hopelessly every second, but all she could do was cling to him and trust him. Everything was a chaos of motion and water. She tried to gulp down air, but accidentally took in some water. She choked, coughed and found herself letting go of his neck.

A wave crashed over her, sending her spinning helplessly back toward the stony shore. She felt herself go head over heels....

Then David's hands were on her body, bearing her up to lightness and air again. He shook her as she sputtered and choked, forcing her to calm herself. Then he made her lock her arms around him as he swam farther out.

Once more, she could only trust him blindly. At last, they reached a place where the water was more peaceful.

He maneuvered her from behind to in front of him, holding her up, treading water. "Tread," he ordered.

She tried to obey although she was exhausted.

"Let's make this fast," he said, his voice raised so she could hear him above the hiss and roar of the water. "Get the pearls."

She tried, but her fingers seemed too weak, too shaky to get hold of them.

"Sorry," he said, breathing hard. "Excuse the familiarity." His hand reached down the front of her bathing suit, fumbling warmly against her chilled breasts. He drew out the soaked bundle of pearls, unwrapped them and let the water tear the handkerchief away.

"Here," he said, his jaw clenched. "Put your hand over mine."

She did, hanging on to his hand as if it were the source of all life. The pearls felt like stones pressed between their tightly joined palms.

"Now," he said, pulling her as closely to him as he could. "Take your hand away from mine. For just a second."

She looked into his eyes in fear and confusion. He nodded. When she hesitated, he nodded again. *Trust me,* he was saying. *Trust me.*

Slowly she drew her hand back. The black pearls slipped into the water. They didn't make so much as a splash before they vanished into the deep.

This time Piper felt no regrets for the necklace, only the sickening terror of being so far out on such a rough sea. Her temples pounded, her stomach churned and she felt faint.

"Put both arms around my neck again," he commanded.

"I don't think I can go through this again," she moaned, hiding her face against his shoulder.

"You have to," he said, no mercy in his voice. He put one hand on her face, turning it up to his. "Piper, it isn't so bad. Think of it as a challenge."

"I can't," she protested. She stared dazedly up into his eyes. If she didn't drown in the sea, she thought, irrationally, she might drown in his sea-blue eyes.

He set his jaw. "All right. Hang on to me. Watch when you breathe. And this time don't let go."

Weakly, almost drunkenly, she obeyed.

SHE WONDERED AFTERWARD if she had passed out during part of the journey back to shore. That was impossible, she thought; if she'd fainted, she would have let go and drowned. But there were parts she couldn't remember. Her mind, numbed by fear, must have refused to register them.

She remembered hitting the shore with an unpleasant jolt, remembered almost being swept back out, but then David's arms wrapped firmly around her and he managed to wrestle her completely out of the water, to carry her back to the carpet of green sand.

Even on land, she couldn't stop clinging to him. Her eyes were still squeezed shut and she imagined a slight stagger in his step, a limp. But then he lay her down, face up, on the warm and blessedly solid sand. "Are you all right?" he asked, his breathing ragged.

"I think so," she gasped, not caring that she was getting sand in her hair. Once more she had swallowed too much water. She wondered, achingly, if she was going to be sick.

David stretched out on his stomach beside her, resting his head on his folded arms. "I'm starting to hate that wizard myself."

Piper rolled over slightly. The sun beat down, bathing her in its life-giving warmth, while the wind blew over her wet body, trying to chill her.

She reached over to touch his shoulder in gratitude, then blinked in surprise.

His shoulder was bloody.

She raised herself on her elbow and stared at him. His arm was cut, as well, and there was blood on his leg.

"David?" she whispered. "Are you all right?"

He raised his face and his eyes met hers. "I'm fine. A little winded, that's all."

"You're bleeding," she said. Tentatively she touched his scraped shoulder.

"So what?" he muttered, and sat up.

Her hand remained resting tentatively on his flesh. He looked at it, then at her.

"You got hurt," she said. "When? How?"

He tossed wet hair out of his eyes. He brushed her hand away. "There at the end. You got panicky in the surf. I had to do a few acrobatics to keep you with me."

"You smashed into the lava," she said in horror. "Let me get some tissues. Oh, David, your leg's really bleeding. And it's because of me. I'm sorry."

She began to rummage through her bag for clean tissues. "Forget it," he said. "It isn't the first time I ever bled. Oouf." He reached over, took his magenta shirt, tore a few strips from it and wrapped it firmly around the gash in his calf.

"You should clean that first," she said, taking a handful of tissues and trying to dab at his shoulder.

"With what?" he said sarcastically. "We don't have water. Sea water won't do any good. Here, give me that. Your hands are still shaking."

He took the tissues from her and pressed them against his shoulder, his scraped bicep and then a cut on his side.

Piper knelt beside him, trembling and feeling guilty. "I don't have a scratch on me. You took all those cuts to save me."

He gave her a short speculative glance. "I think you'll have a few scars, all right. Up here." He reached over and tapped her unceremoniously on the temple.

"I'm sorry," she repeated. "I can't tell you how sorry I am."

He grimaced slightly as he wiped the cut on his side again. "Lord, Piper, why are you so scared of the ocean? I told you you could trust me. We made it just fine, didn't we?"

"You're bleeding in at least four places and I feel sick. I'm not sure my knees will ever support me again. You call that fine?"

He shook his head and his mouth crooked downward. "We would have been fine if you hadn't been so scared.

Why? You said you never saw an ocean until three days ago. How can it frighten you so much? I don't understand.''

She sank back to a sitting position. She stared down at the green sand.

She felt his eyes on her and bent her head, not wanting to meet them. He was right. If she had done as he said, nothing would have happened. She wouldn't have been swept away, she wouldn't have struggled against him, he wouldn't have been hurt. Why had she been so deeply frightened when he had told her not to be? Nothing had ever frightened her before, nothing except lizards and snakes. She was ashamed.

"I don't know," she said at last. Her wet hair hung in her eyes, and her lips and mouth burned from the saltwater. She was weak with thirst, her throat scratchy.

A cold shudder ran through her, then another. She knew she looked terrible, but she didn't care. Nothing mattered except that she had failed David.

He was silent. "Oh, come here," he said at last. He reached over and drew her into his arms. He lay her head against his chest. "You look like a drowned little cat."

It was hardly a compliment, but she didn't care. She leaned against the sun-heated hardness of his shoulder and bit down on her lower lip.

He stroked her hair into place. "Hey," he said, "you can't feel bad. You're perfect, remember?"

She had hardly been perfect in the ocean. She had been fearful, dependent, panicky and now, because of it, he was injured. Once more tears stung her eyes, and this time she was too tired to fight them.

"No," he said, his voice going taut. "No. Don't cry. No. No. No."

Piper couldn't help it. She put her arms around his neck and let the tears fall. "I was so *scared*," she said bitterly.

"I'm never scared. I can't be. I *can't*. I have to take care of the others."

His arms tightened around her. He lay his cheek against her damp hair. "Everybody's scared of something. Don't cry. Don't."

"I was a coward," she sobbed, detesting herself. "Yesterday and even worse today. Why? I've always been brave until now. Why? I've always been strong. Always."

"Shhh," he said, smoothing her hair again. "Don't try to figure it out now. Figure it out later."

"I was even a coward on the plane," she said, trying to burrow more deeply against his shoulder. Her voice shook with disgust. "That never happened before. It's like every time I think of that ocean, it's like a person who's beautiful but dangerous, like a terrible god."

"Good Lord," he said, shaking his head. "Gods in the sea? You make a proper little pagan."

"It frightens me. What's wrong with me?"

He sighed in exasperation, his face grim. He held her, but he didn't try to touch her in any other way. "Nothing's wrong with you," he said. "Nothing at all."

He let her cry it out. Then he wiped her eyes with the last of the clean tissues. He released her and stood, looking down. "Brush your hair," he ordered. "Put on your clothes."

Piper nodded, too tired to argue. He turned away from her. She pulled on her pink sweater, hastily brushed her hair and put lip gloss on her dried lips. She hid her reddened eyes behind her sunglasses.

She put on her slacks, strapped on her ruined sandals. Then she sat on the piece of driftwood a moment, her head down, staring at the green sand and breathing hard.

What had gotten into her lately? she wondered. She had never been a fearful or panicky person. Now she had compounded her shame by weeping in David Whitewater's arms.

Worse, he had been atypically kind and let her. She felt shaky and vulnerable.

She looked up and saw him standing, staring out to sea. He wore his jeans and running shoes, but carried his ruined shirt, crumpled into a ball. He had tied another strip of it around his injured bicep. His back was broad and brown, his waist and hips lean, and his dark hair tossed in the wind.

For a moment, Piper could imagine him in another time, another place. She could see him standing on a rise of land in Nebraska or the Dakotas, bare-chested, his eyes staring out to the horizon. For years, the Indians in the history books had seemed like characters out of myth. Now, suddenly, they seemed real, human, blood of David's blood. Their heritage was his, the one he fought for.

She shook away the fancy and walked to his side. "I'm sorry," she said, her voice almost prim. "Everything's affected me unexpectedly. These islands are off-putting—they can steal your mind, and maybe your soul. I won't let it happen again. Sorry to be such a . . . so undependable."

He turned and gazed down at her, his eyes narrowed lazily. "Dependable Piper. Responsible Piper. Strong little Piper who always does what has to be done. But it's all right. You look perfect again." His eyes flicked down to her battered shoes, then back to her face and her windburned cheeks. Mockery curved his mouth. "At least, almost perfect."

Piper looked away. She didn't want to talk about what had happened anymore.

In silence they walked the long path back to the car. Piper had no idea what David was thinking as he limped beside her. She hardly knew what she herself was thinking. At first she had been drunk on fear and then regret. Now she felt drunk on wind and space and isolation. She could think clearly of nothing except the rolling green hills studded with lava cinders, the plunging glassy blue waves.

When they reached the car at last, David opened the door for her. Gratefully she got inside and leaned back against the civilized softness of the seat.

He got in beside her and put the car into gear. His face and chest and shoulders were sun- and wind-burnished, and his hair hung over his brow. A smear of dry blood darkened the flesh just beneath the strip of cloth. Neither of them spoke as the car started its journey up the hill.

On the way down to the sea, they had seen no one along the road. Except for a few grazing cattle, the countryside had been deserted. Now, just as they passed a pasture near a quiet farmhouse, Piper noticed a teenage girl.

The girl stood under the shade of a ohia tree. She wore jeans and a red halter, and a black Stetson hat hid her eyes. Her long hair was a startlingly pale blond and danced in the wind. By her side was a smooth-haired white dog with drooping ears.

For a moment the girl seemed to watch them. Then she turned and disappeared behind a rise of land. The white dog stood staring out at the road. Then it, too, turned and ran over the rise, vanishing with a wag of its long tail.

Piper swallowed hard, a knot in her dry throat. She thought of what Mrs. Lilola had said. Pele could take any form: young or old, fair or dark. And she had a little white dog.

She glanced at David, whose face wore its now familiar unreadable expression.

Without looking at her, he reached over and squeezed her hand. His touch made her heart hammer even harder. "Don't worry about it," he said. "It's coincidence. Don't go superstitious on me."

Then he took his hand away. He said no more of the incident. Neither did she.

CHAPTER EIGHT

THE NEXT PART of the ceremony was to take place on the island of Maui. That meant another flight over the ocean, and Piper gritted her teeth the whole way, even though the trip was smooth.

From the plane, Maui seemed an almost blinding green. The sugar fields of its great valley gleamed as brilliantly as emeralds.

David rented a car as Piper looked about the airport, her fifth in three days. When David drove them to their hotel in the coastal village of Lahaina, she numbly watched the countryside. Sights flowed by, exotic and lovely, but her brain was already overloaded. They rode in silence.

David wore a short-sleeved white knit shirt, black jeans and cowboy boots. When he walked, he limped slightly. A bandage shone whitely against the brown of his bicep. Nothing else gave indication that earlier in the day he had been battling the surf, trying to keep her from being battered against the rocks.

Piper's beige dress was full skirted and cut with elegant simplicity. Her high-heeled sandals matched, as did her gold-clasped purse. Now, as they drove along the ocean-front highway, she could feel David's eyes glancing toward her frequently.

"What's wrong?" she asked irritably, keeping her own eyes on the scenery. She was still ashamed of the way she had acted at the green sand beach, and she was not, she found, above taking it out on him.

"You don't look like somebody who nearly hiked to death, then got tossed around in the sea like a rag doll. Aren't you sore? Tired? Hungry?"

"I'm all of those," she said, still not looking at him. She rested her elbow on the car window and her chin on her fist.

"Sorry," he said, his voice derisive. "You just don't look sore, tired or hungry."

"Appearances, as my grandmother always says, are everything."

"Appearances, as my grandfather always used to say, are deceiving."

"Maybe we can combine the two," she said flippantly. "Deception is everything."

"Let's not. You're too much that way already."

She spun to face him. "I'm *not* deceptive. I happen to be an honest ethical person."

He shrugged his injured shoulder. "To other people maybe. Not always to yourself."

She frowned in puzzlement.

"Ah," he said with an air of triumph. "Something's been bothering me. Now I know. Earrings. You don't have on earrings, ones that match everything."

Piper turned from him and stared moodily out the window again. "I was going to wear the gold ones. I lost one somewhere today."

"Today? Where?"

"I don't know," she said with bitterness. "Maybe a wave knocked it out. Maybe the wind blew it out. Maybe a fish gnawed it out. At any rate, it's lost, and I'll have to pay my grandmother for it."

"What?" he asked, raising an eyebrow.

"She doesn't give jewelry away," Piper said, watching the seaside trees nod in the wind. "She loans it."

Somehow, she thought, he managed to make even silence sarcastic.

She gave him a reproving look. "She's always been careful not to overindulge me. I told you—she won't buy affection."

"I see."

"Look," Piper said impatiently. "I thought we weren't going to snipe at each other's families. Tell me what else we have to do today. Do you dangle me over a volcano crater by my heels?"

"Not until tomorrow. We'll check into the hotel, eat, then make a visit."

Piper sighed. "Another volcano priestess? The last one made me feel two inches tall. And I still don't know what she was getting at with that story about the Cloud Holders."

David's fugitive smile appeared, the first time since they'd left the beach. "You weren't supposed to understand. She wanted to mystify you."

Piper didn't respond. She felt mystified, all right. She was no longer sure how she felt about the necklace, David, or anything else. She wished she could talk to Eloise, who would help put her thoughts in order.

At times like this, when Piper was tired or upset, she found herself pondering the story of the Cloud Holders. What had it meant? That love could destroy you? Or that it made you whole? That you lost yourself in it? Or found yourself? That it would hurt you? Or heal you?

Oh, why am I thinking about love? she wondered wearily. Eloise had always made love sound dangerous. Never had there been a man in the history of the family who could be trusted and depended upon. What good was love?

MRS. LETTIE OPUA was a diminutive woman in her sixties who looked part Oriental, part Hawaiian. The living room of her tidy house in Lahaina was a shrine to children and grandchildren. Framed pictures of various sizes hung on every wall, stood on every surface.

Lettie Opua poured them each a cup of tea and urged them to help themselves to macadamia-nut cookies. "So this Portuguese sorcerer left all these complicated instructions about the necklace," she said. "How interesting. I've never heard such a thing before."

"Mrs. Opua," David said, picking up his cup, "the instructions say we're supposed to talk to three priestesses about Pele. Do you have any idea why? What it is we're supposed to learn?"

The woman smiled and gave a humorous shrug. "First, I never called myself a priestess. But if a kahuna is an expert, then, yes, I might be considered a kahuna of the humblest sort. I'm only a teacher who's made a little study of such things."

Piper took a deep breath of relief. Unlike Mary Lilola, Mrs. Opua seemed friendly, interested, cooperative and down-to-earth. "What do you think we're supposed to be told?"

Mrs. Opua looked thoughtful. "I've wondered ever since the Cultural Bureau contacted me."

"And?" David probed. The delicate tea cup seemed dwarfed by his strong hand.

She sighed. "Perhaps the best thing to tell you is the most basic. I have no secret knowledge, no mystical message. The Hawaiian beliefs about life and death were very complicated, very sophisticated actually. But the missionaries didn't like them and tried to stamp them out."

"Yes?" Piper said, nodding. Beside her, David had become solemn, even brooding.

"Like the ancient Greeks and Romans, the Hawaiians had many gods," the woman went on. "Some families traced their ancestry to these gods—including Pele. Family was, and still is, extremely important to Hawaiians. In the old days, they believed family members who died went to eternity and became godly. They turned into guardian spirits of the family and were revered, looked upon as great forces.''

She paused. "Forgive me. I make this sound simple when it's complex.''

"Go on, Mrs. Opua," David urged. "At this point we probably couldn't understand anything except a simplified version."

She smiled. "Well, by tradition, a dead loved one was transformed into a guardian spirit through a ceremony. A person given the volcano ceremony would be transformed into a flame spirit, who could come back and help its relatives or punish people who had been bad."

Piper shifted uncomfortably. She didn't want to entertain the thought of ghosts who punished.

"They also believed in a person's mana, in a power that connects him with the supernatural. A person's mana is in his body, but also in his possessions, unless he passes them on to a relative. So upon death, a person should take his mana with him into eternity."

David nodded. "You're saying that to rob the dead would be to rob part of their spiritual power, to keep them bound to earth?"

"Something like that," she agreed. "Such a spirit, kept back, might become confused and do evil."

Piper's uneasiness grew. "Do people still believe this?"

Mrs. Opua's brow furrowed and she shrugged. "Who can look into someone's heart and say what he truly believes? How many of the old feelings linger? It's hard to say. People are reluctant to discuss such things."

"But," David said, still solemn, "by following the proper ritual, a stolen or borrowed relic could be returned? The spirit of the relative set free?"

"Yes." Mrs. Opua nodded. "Such a ceremony is called *kaku'ai.*"

Piper fidgeted again. She wanted nothing to do with strange gods and stranger ceremonies. "That's what we're supposed to be performing?"

"According to the documents concerning your wizard," Mrs. Opua said. She paused. "Although it's not the usual ceremony. It's not really Hawaiian."

Piper shook her head, troubled. "But people still believe in Pele's power?"

"Ah," said Mrs. Opua with a thoughtful sigh. "Pele. Go up near Hana, to the ruins of the old temple. You'll see offerings to her. Go to the Big Island, to the crater. You'll find more. And not all are from Hawaiians. Yes. People still believe in her."

"Do you believe in her?" Piper asked boldly.

The woman's expression did not change. "I believe we should respect one another's beliefs. What do you believe, my dear?"

Piper shrugged, feeling vaguely guilty. "Even if it involves sacrificing something valuable? Something worth money?"

"My dear, my dear," said Mrs. Opua kindly, shaking her head. "You have never been a member of an oppressed people. Nothing is more valuable than respect. Nothing."

Piper sank a bit deeper into the couch. "Well," she said lamely, "the money could be used to help people."

Mrs. Opua stared at her a long moment, amusement mingling with sadness on her face. "Oh, Miss Gordon," she murmured, "what greater help can people have than to keep their self-respect? And the respect of others for their traditions?"

David gave Piper a long measuring sidelong glance. *Do you understand yet?* his eyes asked.

And for that she had no answer. She did not know.

ELOISE'S TRAVEL AGENT must have slipped up; their hotel rooms in Lahaina had views of the sea. They were small rooms, but their glass sliding doors opened onto railed balconies that overlooked the Pacific.

Piper slept with the balcony doors open and the warm flower-scented breeze blowing over her. She awoke to a room awash in sunlight and to the purr of the surf. She blinked, sighed with pleasure and snuggled more deeply into the crisp sheets.

White sheets, white wallpaper, white curtains blowing in the breeze. The world seemed bright and pure, wind-washed and without stain.

She rose and stretched in the sunlight spilling through the open doors. Her nightgown was also white and it billowed like a delicate cloud, just grazing her ankles. She stepped out onto the balcony to gaze at the sea.

From this distance, she thought, the ocean didn't look dangerous. The sky was a bright and tender blue, the sea a quiet blue-gray, and in the distance, directly before her, was another island, like a great gray-green shadow, half-cloaked by clouds. It was the island of Lanai, David had told her the previous evening, and to her left, the island of Molokai.

Piper leaned on the railing and inhaled the clean air deeply. Birds twittered in the foliage somewhere, and white spray tossed on the glittering water.

What a beautiful country, she thought. *What a paradise. What if I stayed? What if I never went home?*

Don't be silly, she told herself sternly. Eloise needed her. Eloise was depending on her; the whole family was.

She turned from the railing and went inside again, feeling oddly sad. For all her inner conflicts, she'd never felt as alive as she did here in Hawaii. At least, she told herself, she understood now why the Portuguese sailor had jumped ship all those years ago: to stay in paradise. Becoming a cut-rate wizard had probably seemed a small price to pay.

She went to the bathroom to shower. As soon as she was clean and dressed, she would try to call Eloise again. She needed to talk to her badly. David Whitewater kept rattling her faith in her opinions, her identity, even her family. Something in the very air of Hawaii seemed to be trying to change her.

She opened the door of the shower stall and glanced idly at white tiled walls.

She screamed.

Four beadlike eyes stared at her. Two green *things*—lizards—clung to the tiles. They had long snakelike tails and bony reptilian faces with snakelike smiles.

She rocketed out of the bathroom, screaming again as she beat on the bedroom wall with her fists.

"Whitewater! Whitewater! Help! Help!"

She heard a sound next door, as if furniture were being knocked over. A door slammed. Somebody beat on her door, then crashed against it.

She ran to the door, unchained the safety lock and flung it open. David stood there, his face tense with concern.

He stepped inside, seizing her by the arms. "What's wrong?" He wore white shorts and an unbuttoned white short-sleeved shirt. She found herself staring at his tanned chest. He squeezed her arms hard, as if trying to assure her he was there and she was safe.

"I-I..." she stammered. "There are creatures in my shower stall!"

His expression of concern mutated into one of distrust. "Creatures?"

"Yes," she said, nodding vigorously. "These serpent things."

One corner of his mouth curled up. The other went down. "Serpent things?"

"Yes," she insisted, "these *lizards* or something."

"Lizards," he said tonelessly. "I just did a broad jump over a bed and knocked over a night table because you saw lizards?"

"David," she said, almost angrily, "there are *reptiles* in the bathroom."

He released her arms and stepped into the bathroom, his face stormy. "Well, after that carrying on, I hope it's at least the Loch Ness monster."

He swung the shower door open. The two lizards looked at him with their evil little eyes. They twitched their scaly tails. Piper, who had followed David, stepped back in revulsion.

David swore. "It's just a couple of chameleons," he said in disgust.

"David, they're *reptiles,* and they're in my *shower,* and I might have gotten in there *with* them and they could have *jumped* on me—"

"That," he said sarcastically, "might have been worth nearly breaking my neck over. You, dressed in nothing but lizards. Begging me to pluck them off."

"Will you just get them out of there?" she asked.

"Yes, ma'am," he answered in an unpleasant parody of obedience. "This is why I spent all those years in law school. To come running at a moment's notice to divest ladies of their lizards. All right, princess. I'll save you from the dragons."

"And don't chase them into the room," Piper ordered.

"Don't give me orders," he ordered back.

She took another step back as he moved toward the chameleons, but he had remarkably quick hands, and with three or four swift movements, he had imprisoned both animals. They stared, bright-eyed and hideous, out of his brown hand.

"Ugh," Piper said.

"They're cute," he said, carrying them out to the balcony. "And they're soft. They feel like velvet."

"David," she pleaded, following him, "take them outside. Please."

"This *is* outside, dammit. They're not going to stay around here. They don't like this any better than you do."

He bent down, reaching through the railing, and placed them on the rough bricks of the wall. For a moment they clung there with their spidery little toes. Then they flicked their tails and scuttled downward, out of sight.

David straightened. He made a restless movement with his wide shoulders before staring at her with annoyance. For an instant his blue eyes flickered to her rounded breasts straining against the white-ribboned bodice of her gown. Then they returned to her face. "You're welcome," he said.

She stared at the wall down which the lizards had disappeared. She found she was breathing hard. "Thank you," she said grudgingly.

"And don't ever scream for me like that again unless the guy from *Psycho* is in your shower."

"I'm sorry," she said. "They startled me. I'm not used to having iguanas jump at me."

"They weren't iguanas and they didn't jump."

"Well, they looked like iguanas to me, and I thought they might jump."

"I'm sitting on the balcony, reading, when you let out this bloodcurdling shriek. Just when Rhett was telling Scarlet to marry him. I hope she's got sense enough to say yes."

Piper sighed in exasperation and budding shame. She turned to face him, then wished she hadn't. He looked too handsome in the early-morning light, his hair tossed by the ocean breeze. His eyes were too blue, his skin too tanned against the white blaze of his opened shirt. His legs were too long and thickly muscled, his shoulders too broad.

"Listen," she said. "I'm sorry. I don't like snaky things. I never have."

He said nothing. He just stood, looking down at her. The breeze rose, rippling his opened shirt, the folds of her white gown.

Self-consciously she turned away, looking beyond the hotel's flowers and grassy lawn, to the glistening tossing sea. "I'm not the sort of woman who screams about bugs and faints over mice. I just dislike . . . cold-blooded things. I always have."

The silence pulsed between them. She tensed. She did not want to look at him again.

"People say I'm cold-blooded," he said, his voice low. "But I like the way you look in white. I like the way the sun shines on your bare shoulders and your hair."

She shuddered slightly and drew her shoulders up, as if to protect herself. The balmy breeze toyed with her hair. She felt him move nearer. Needles of electricity pricked her spine.

"Piper," he said, "turn around. Look at me."

She took a deep breath, and set her jaw. She stared off toward the island of Lanai, stretching mysteriously under its mantle of clouds. Another island, she thought in confusion. Another place I haven't been. Another world I know nothing about. Everything's too mysterious here. Everything's too new.

"Piper, turn and look at me." Something in his tone made her want to shiver in spite of the sunshine pouring down. She stood as still as she could, staring toward the island she didn't know.

She closed her eyes and took another deep breath of clean-washed sea air. She felt the sun warming her face and shoulders and breasts, the breeze softly caressing her.

Opening her eyes, she gazed at Lanai again, almost misty across the sunny harbor. Someday I want to know about that place, too, she thought.

Then, because she could not stop herself from doing so, she turned, raising her eyes to David's. In the depths of his gaze, dark blue fire burned.

He bent toward her, taking her into his arms as naturally as the wind embraces a leaf. A sound, almost a moan, growled deep in his throat.

His warm mouth bore down on hers, questing. He drew her nearer to him, as if he could make their two bodies merge into one if he held her closely enough. All her senses leapt, like flames dancing into life.

Piper felt her arms rising, going around his neck, her hands touching the crisp cloth of his shirt, feeling the warm hardness of his back beneath it. She felt awash in a sea of brightness, of fragrant wind and sunshine and David's dizzying masculine touch.

Her lips parted beneath his and they tasted deeply of each other. One of his hands rose to cradle the back of her head, his fingers lacing through her silky hair. His breathing mingled with hers, warm and pulsing.

His bare chest pressed against her breasts, and she could not tell whose heart she felt pounding so strongly that it shook her. She clung to him more tightly, needing his strength for support, for he was making her weak, half-faint with desire.

"You taste like sunshine," he murmured against her lips. "You taste like morning in paradise." He kissed her again, his tongue dancing against hers. Then his lips moved to her neck, kissing her first beneath the jaw, then at the sensitive hollow of her throat.

Somehow he had moved her to the doorway and the gauzy white curtains were blowing on either side of them.

David ran his hands down, then up her bare arms. He took her lips again.

He turned her to kiss her more deeply, and somehow they had stepped within the room, so now the curtains fluttered around them in white billows, tangling, then untangling about their bodies, fluttering in the sun.

Piper gasped, as if breathless from some giddy intoxicating waltz. She tried to take a hesitant step away from him, but he followed, hands running up and down her arms again, caressing her shoulders, drawing her back to him.

She was being enchanted, she thought tipsily, bewitched by the morning's clean dazzle, by his expert mouth teaching hers new secrets, by the strength of his arms and the heat of his tall body.

He kissed her throat, then her mouth again, his tongue caressing hers. Piper closed her eyes, not wanting to resist him. She felt as if she were falling through space.

Then, somehow, they were on the edge of her unmade bed, then on it, lying in the crisp and snowy tumble of the sheets. David's white shirt was off, and he lay, bare-chested, bending over her, one hand pushing down the strap of her gown, his lips hot against the curve of her breast.

She drew her hands along his shoulders and arms, exploring the ropy working of his muscles, the smoothness of his bare skin, the rough spots where the lava rock had scraped him.

"This is crazy," he said against her throat. "We've got to stop."

"I know," she said, and kissed the hard curve of his jaw.

He pushed down her other strap. He kissed her ear. "Make me stop," he said, his voice ragged, his breath warm in her ear.

"I can't," she said, her lips against the heat of his wind-burned shoulder.

"Piper..." His mouth found the warm valley between her breasts. His lips and tongue began to make her feel half crazed, half spellbound.

She tried to draw away from him, but found she could not. It wasn't simply sex she wanted; she wanted to be as close as possible to David Whitewater, to touch and be touched by this man and no other. She wanted to explore every secret intimacy with him because he was David, dark, intense, paradoxical David, and somehow she was falling in love with him.

Love? she thought with a pang of fear. She couldn't love him. He was her grandmother's enemy. Eloise hated this man. And he hated Eloise.

The phone rang, a shrill mechanical blast that rent the air like a warning.

"Don't answer it," he said.

A bolt of panic shot through her. Her body tautened, and her mind numbed with apprehension. "What if it's my grandmother?"

The phone rang again.

He raised his head; his hair was tousled, but his expression was almost rigid with willpower. "Your grandmother?" His hands on her went suddenly still.

Piper lay, staring into his jewel-blue eyes, her heart beating crazily. What would Eloise say if she knew that at this moment Piper was in bed with David Whitewater? She remembered Eloise's voice shaking with bitterness: *Never forget who you are. And never forget what that man did to us.*

David had persecuted Eloise in court, he had forced her to give up the necklace, and now he was destroying it. Why did Piper desire so deeply to be in his arms? With disquiet she recalled Mrs. Lilola's words: "Love pushes in opposite directions."

Again the phone ground out its jarring note. Warily she watched his face, and he watched hers. The muscle twitched in his cheek, once, twice, then flickered under control. Piper ran the tip of her tongue nervously over the edge of her upper lip.

He watched the motion hungrily, but he did not bend to kiss her again.

She raised herself slightly, reaching for the phone. His hands still grasped her upper arms, and the warmth of his touch and his nearness made her breathless.

But she picked up the receiver, her eyes still on his. "Hello," she managed to say, hoping she sounded normal.

The only answer was a buzzing hum. No one was there.

For some reason the sound unnerved her more than Eloise's voice could have. "Hello?" she said again, and this time she heard the tremor in her voice. "Hello?"

Only the accusing hum replied. Her muscles stiffened, but she and David remained staring into each other's eyes. She knew he, too, could hear the sound, the empty angry buzz. She put down the receiver and looked away from him, suddenly frightened.

What if it hadn't been Eloise at all? Piper thought. What if it had been something far more mysterious, sending its rage through the phone wires because they were about to defy the ritual? No, she told herself, such a thought was madness. The caller had to have been Eloise, it had to. Goddesses didn't resort to phone calls.

Slowly David let his hands drop from her. He raised himself to sit on the edge of the bed, turning his broad back to her. She glanced at him nervously. He ran his hand over his hair with an angry movement. His voice came from between clenched teeth.

"Get dressed. I'll meet you down in the lobby. I'll take the coral out of the necklace in the manager's office."

She sat up, too, selfconscious and oddly hurt. She pulled the crinkling sheet to cover her nearly bared breasts. Her body still throbbed with the forbidden enchantment of his touch.

He glanced over his shoulder at her, then turned away once more. "I don't want to be alone in this room with you again," he said in the same bitter tone. "And I don't want you in mine."

"I see," she said with false calm. But she didn't see. Had he felt the same jolt of superstitious fear as she had? No, she thought, not David. He was the man whose universe centered on logic.

He stood and picked up his shirt with a motion of disgust. "We've got a ritual to get through. It's got that interesting chastity clause. I'm the guy who's supposed to see that everything's done by the rules. Once we've fulfilled the requirements of the ritual, then, if you still want a roll in the hay, we can give it a try."

She pulled up the straps of her gown, drew the tangled sheet more tightly around herself. She glared at him in pain and anger. What had been happening between them had felt beautiful and natural to her. He made it sound cheap.

"And where are you going?" she asked, forcing herself to sound flippant. "To get a sledgehammer to smash the coral, oh peerless guardian of the necklace?"

"I'm going to take a shower," he said, giving her a fierce glance. "A cold one."

He left her sitting in the white jumble of sheets, the sunlight streaming through the opened doors, the white curtains blowing emptily in the wind.

CHAPTER NINE

THE PHONE RANG AGAIN shortly after David left the room. With trepidation, Piper lifted the receiver, half-expecting the scold of the anonymous buzz again.

She was relieved to hear Eloise's brisk voice. "Hello. Let's keep this short. The phone rates are astronomical."

"Oh," Piper said, breathing easier. "I've tried and tried to get you. Is something wrong?"

There was a moment of silence that made Piper apprehensive. "Everything's fine," Eloise replied at last. "I was in the hospital, but I'm home again, feeling better—and as mean as ever."

"The hospital?" Piper cried. "You were in the hospital? Nobody told me?"

"It was nothing," Eloise insisted with a sniff. "Chest pains. They put me in for observation. I told Harold and Jeannie I'd skin them alive if they called you. I'm *fine*. It was nothing but fatigue and nerves. They're giving me vitamin shots. And new medication for my gout. I'm actually far better than when you left."

"I'm coming home right now," Piper said. "Why didn't you tell me? When did this happen?"

"Piper, settle down and stay where you are. You have a job to do. Nothing's wrong. It happened during your flight to Hawaii. What could you have done?"

"I hope it wasn't this idiocy about the necklace that put you in the hospital," Piper said with passion. "I hope it wasn't that David Whitewater—"

"No, no, no," Eloise said impatiently. "It'll take more than some half-breed upstart to put me in my grave."

Piper winced.

"Maybe there's something to this necklace nonsense, after all," Eloise said, her voice wry. "I really am much better. And I have good news." She paused. "Very good news. To me. And I hope to you."

"Yes?" Piper said, puzzled.

There was another moment of silence.

"MacDowell's come home."

Piper, sitting on the edge of the bed, felt slightly stunned. A dozen different emotions tried to crowd into her mind, but none registered except perturbed surprise.

"MacDowell's home?" she asked carefully. "In Nebraska?"

Eloise's tone was wryer than before. "I told Jeannie not to call you. It never occurred to me to tell her not to call MacDowell. He came right away."

"How wonderful," Piper said softly. "I know how much you've missed him."

"Piper, he's talking about staying."

"Staying?" Piper swallowed hard. All her life she'd been trained to take over the responsibilities MacDowell had shrugged off.

"Staying," Eloise repeated with satisfaction. "He's a widower now. His stepsons are grown. He's run his own business for years and made a success of it. He's proved he can make it on his own. So now he's ready to come home. To his family. Where he belongs."

"How wonderful," Piper said, but she felt a frightening emptiness in her heart. Would Eloise need her any longer if MacDowell came home? Would anybody?

"Jeannie's in seventh heaven," Eloise said with satisfaction. "MacDowell could always manage her better than anyone. And I think it's just what Harold needs. A male example. Maybe he'll develop a little gumption. He's quite, quite taken with MacDowell. And MacDowell has some excellent ideas about providing for the twins.''

"How wonderful," Piper said again, but the words sounded even more hollow in her ears than before. "And he's thinking of ... managing the business for you, too?"

There was another beat of silence. "You can help him manage things, just as you help me," Eloise replied. "MacDowell is very competent. Experienced. I've felt guilty about you, Piper. I've kept you working too hard for too long. You can finally have some freedom.''

"I—I see," said Piper. But she felt wounded and more than a little betrayed. How could MacDowell come waltzing back into their lives after all these years, taking over her job, her place in the family, almost her very identity?

"Piper, I realize this probably makes you feel a bit strange, but you know that you're special to me and that I love you.''

"Of course," Piper said mechanically. "I love you, too."

"I don't love you any less because MacDowell's come home. You understand that, don't you? I've prayed for this for years, that someday he'd see the light.''

Suddenly Piper felt ashamed of herself for resenting MacDowell. Eloise was happy, and that was what was important. Jeannie was happy, too, and so, apparently, was Harold. Even the twins might be better off. "I'm glad for you," she said, and that much, at least, she could say with feeling.

Eloise chatted a moment about Harold and his wife, claiming that if they would stop being so jittery about the baby, it would probably arrive with no further delay.

Then her voice became sarcastic. She sounded almost like her old self. "And how's our gallant Sioux brave? I hope you're leading him a merry dance. I love the idea of him chasing himself all over Hawaii.''

Something within Piper seemed to wither. "I—I'm glad it's almost over."

"So am I," said Eloise. "It's costing me a fortune. Well, don't let him get too familiar with you. Don't ever forget what that man did to us. Make him remember who we are."

But who are we? Piper wanted to plead. Nobody he respects. What difference does it make how fine our family is or how far back it goes? What difference?

Instead she said, "Did you call me a little while ago?" She remembered the mysterious phone call that had interrupted her and David, and desperately she wanted Eloise to say, "Yes."

"No," Eloise said. "I was talking to MacDowell. Why?"

"I—I—" Piper began, then stopped. She couldn't tell Eloise. She must never tell anyone.

Eloise chatted a moment longer, clucking once again about how outrageous the long-distance rates were, then hung up.

Piper sat, staring at nothing in particular. She told herself it was wonderful for Eloise that MacDowell had come back into the fold after all these years. It was almost a miracle—for Eloise. But what changes would it wreak in Piper's carefully planned life? She felt shaken, as if the earth itself had suddenly shifted beneath her, no longer solid.

"YOU SHOULD HAVE BROUGHT something heavier than that froufrou," David said with a disdainful glance at the fuzzy pink sweater she held in her lap.

They were driving up the mountainside switchbacks, toward the Haleakala Crater. It was the first thing he'd said to her since the trip had begun.

She smoothed the sweater defensively. "I just stood in the manager's office and watched you smash about a hundred dollars worth of black coral to smithereens," she said, keeping her voice even. "Could you just let me alone?"

"Ah," he gibed. "You're talking money again. You sound like your old self. You must have talked to your grandmother."

"Would it be possible for you to be quiet?" she asked, staring out the window. "I'd be willing to sacrifice diamonds for that."

He shrugged, not bothering to look at her. He turned on the radio. Mellow Hawaiian music crooned.

Piper sighed, not feeling in the least mellow. She tried to sort out her feelings over two separate crises: what was happening with MacDowell back in Nebraska, and what had almost happened with David Whitewater here. Both filled her with a mixture of confusion, insecurity and resentment.

"This place gives me a headache," she said, staring gloomily out the window. "It's always changing. It's like living in a kaleidoscope."

Lahaina, half an hour behind them, had been lush and tropical. Now, they had entered a drier, sterner zone, with stretches of eerily green grass and twisted trees.

"Please," David said, "spare me. Nobody complains about Hawaiian scenery."

"Well, it keeps you off balance," she retorted. "What do I have to do when we get to the top of this thing? Fling myself into the volcano fire?"

"Alas, no," he answered out of the side of his mouth. "It's dormant. No fire for centuries."

"Then what's the fuss about it?" Piper demanded. "What good's a dormant volcano? You can see those anywhere."

"Not like this one."

"I see. Wonders and miracles await us."

"A few. Whether you can see them is another matter."

"Is that another remark about my general inadequacy? My spiritual blindness?"

"It's a remark about the weather. It'll be cold up there. And probably cloudy."

"If it's cloudy, why do they call it the House of the Sun?" she challenged.

"I see you've been reading postcards again. Well, pursue your education any way you can, that's my philosophy."

"So I read it on a postcard. What do you care?"

He switched off the radio. He set his jaw. "All right. What is it? It's this morning, isn't it? You're upset about this morning."

"I most certainly am not," she lied. "You caught me with my defenses down and tried to take advantage of me. I have nothing to be ashamed of."

"What?" He almost barked the word at her.

Unsettled, Piper stared out the window. The landscape had changed again. The sky had grown gray and cloudy, and the earth had turned into a sort of autumnal scrubland, stone scattered with dull green and orange vegetation.

"I wasn't myself because of the lizards," she insisted. "It was the lizards, that's all."

"If lizards have that effect on women, remind me always to carry a couple."

She turned to face him, trying to quell him with a hostile glance. "I'm telling the truth. You caught me at a disadvantage, that's all."

He drew in his breath harshly and struck the steering wheel with the flat of his hand. "You sound exactly the way your grandmother did in court—twisting everything to excuse yourself. For once in your life could you face reality? Could you once face things the way they are?"

"I see things *exactly* as they are." Drizzle was speckling the glass.

"No." With an angry motion he switched on the windshield wipers. "You don't. It was lust, not lizards. Plain old-fashioned lust. You and I have been caged up together too long. We had a natural basic animal reaction. That's all it was. Call it by its right name.'' He struck the steering wheel again.

Piper turned away. She felt as if he had thrust a knife into her. He had called it lust. She had wanted to call it something else. She supposed she had wanted to call it love, even though love was impossible between them.

"And," he said, his voice almost a growl, "you're never going to admit your precious grandmother might be guilty in that Navaho-jewelry business. And that I might be right. If she was innocent, why didn't she appeal to a higher court? Because she *knew* she was guilty. Don't tell me you see things as they are. You never have, and you probably never will. If I put cold hard undeniable proof in front of your nose, you'd say it wasn't there."

"Maybe she didn't appeal it because she didn't want to face *you* again," Piper said angrily, believing it was true. "I wouldn't blame her. Leave me alone. Just leave me alone."

THE JOURNEY FROM LAHAINA to the great Haleakala Crater was like a climb upward through the seasons, Piper thought numbly. It began in the exuberant luxury of summer, then turned to green vistas streaked with gold, then to a rough landscape as gray and brown and yellow as a Nebraska October. At last, at the summit, winter ruled the land. It was cold, barren and gray, a magnificent wasteland, and its desolation mirrored Piper's feelings.

When Piper and David finally arrived at Haleakala, the House of the Sun was sunless, freezing and encased in cloud. Theirs was the only car in the black-paved parking lot. Piper looked about, bewildered. "Where is everybody? I thought this was a tourist attraction."

"There are weather warnings for this part of the island. Maybe everybody stayed home."

She shivered. Mist dotted the windshield. By the time they reached the high and stony part of the mountain she had slipped into her sweater and David had turned on the car's heater. She hated to admit that he'd been right; her flimsy sweater would not be adequate.

He reached into the back seat and handed her his sweat-shirt. "Here. Put this on. You'll need it."

She looked at him warily. He wore jeans, running shoes and a long-sleeved blue T-shirt almost the same shade as his eyes. "What about you?" she asked.

"I'm not important in this drama. I'm just a spear car-rier. You're the one who's got to last out there."

She wiggled into the sweatshirt and pulled up its hood. David opened his side of the car and a cold blast of air pierced through her. She grimaced. How could Hawaii be this cold?

Before she could think of a rational answer, another blast of frigid air shook her. David had opened the door on her side and was practically hauling her out of the car. "Hurry up," he ordered. "It's freezing."

The world had turned into an eerie landscape of black and gray: black pavement, black chunks of lava, black sand and swirling gray clouds.

Gray mist closed around her, penetrating her clothes, her flesh, her bones. The cold cut like a razor.

Shivering, she looked up at David, who frowned with discomfort. "Why's it so cold?" she asked, wanting to dart back to the warmth of the car.

"Because we're ten thousand feet above sea level," he said, drawing her toward a black path. "Let's get this show on the road."

Piper wanted to look about, but had to duck her head against the assault of the cold. David half-led, half-pulled her up the cindery path. Great chunks of black lava edged the path, which led to a one-storied structure perched phantom-like at the edge of a steep cliff.

"Here," David said, handing her a small bundle. "It's what's left of the coral. Let's get up there, toss it, and get out."

Her fingers were so cold they could barely close around the package. It was not simply the bitter cold, she thought, her teeth chattering, it was the damp, as well. David's thin shirt was already molding itself damply to his muscles. In spite of herself she clung to his arm, eager for any hint of warmth.

Her heart began to pound and she found that she was panting. David turned and gazed down at her. "Altitude getting you?"

"I guess," she gasped, the pulse in her temples nearly deafening her. When he took her hand, she let him, grateful for the warmth of his touch.

"All right," he said, wincing against the rising wind. "We'll take it slow."

"I can't take it slow," Piper protested, shuddering. "I'll freeze to death. If it's a choice between freezing and having my heart burst, I'd just as soon go fast."

He slowed anyway, and when she didn't stop shuddering, he wrapped an arm around her. "Do I need a lizard to do this?" he asked between clenched teeth.

She wanted to tell him she hated him, but she couldn't spare the breath. They reached the little observation station, and Piper looked down into the crater. All she could see was a swiftly dropping wall of black rubble that disappeared in shifting cloaks of mist.

At the edge of the mist stood a brown sign. In yellow letters it said STAY BACK. In white letters it said STEEP CLIFF. Beyond it the world fell away.

"Here?" Piper asked, shivering against him.

He pulled her tighter to him, needing her warmth, she suspected, as much as she needed his. He shrugged. "It's as good as anywhere."

She squared her shoulders and leaned against him. Her heart banged in her chest, and her fingers were frozen. The mist was soaking through her clothing, boring through her like a thousand icy needles.

She was too cold and breathless to speak. Clouds rolled around them like a sea. Nothing in the world seemed solid any longer, except for the black patch of stone on which she stood and the tall man beside her.

"Here," David said, hunching his shoulders against the cold. "Let's try it here."

The wind had risen, almost whipping away his words. When Piper's numb fingers fumbled, trying to undo the crushed coral, David put his arms around her from behind. He helped her untie the handkerchief that bound the fragments.

"Now," he said in her ear.

She stood on the edge of the abyss. The wind came like a polar ghost, chilling her through, but she felt David's arms around her, holding her steadfast, secure. Opening the handkerchief, she let the wind sweep away the ruined coral. Its chips disappeared into the swirling gray. The handkerchief flapped in the wind, white and empty. The coral was gone.

"Let's go," David said in her ear, "before we turn to ice."

By now her clothing was wet, and her face numb with cold. She followed him, her hand in his, almost stumbling as they made their way back down the steep path to the car.

"Get in," he said, almost pushing her inside to the warmth. She collapsed against the seat, breathing heavily. In a few seconds he was beside her, slamming shut his door. He turned on the ignition and switched on the heater.

He looked at her and smiled.

She could hardly bear to look at him. He had a dazzling smile when he chose to use it, white and nearly irresistible with its one-sided dimple. His hair was damp, his face dark with cold, and his T-shirt clung to him, dark with freezing moisture. What did he have to smile about?

"You never believe me about anything," he said. "Next time I tell you to dress for the cold, will you listen? You're blue. You look nice blue, but not particularly happy."

She wasn't sure her jaws would work. "You demon," she managed to say between shudders. "I've nearly drowned in the ocean. I've nearly been blown away off the Kona coast. Now I'm half-frozen. Tomorrow I probably *will* fall into the volcano and die."

"Maybe I should find a lizard. I could warm you up."

Piper shivered in her sodden layers of clothing, in no mood to be teased. As they pulled out of the parking lot, she idly noticed another car in the mist at its edge. She hadn't seen it before. It must have arrived when they were on the path.

She glimpsed a black-haired woman in red inside the vehicle. Oddly, for all the clouds outside, the woman's eyes were hidden by dark glasses. In the passenger seat, its paws against the window, stood a cream-colored poodle. Piper felt a chill deeper than the crater's cold.

Clouds hid the other car from her sight when she tried to look back. *Don't be ridiculous,* she told herself. *It was only another tourist, that's all.*

David cast her a speculative glance, and she knew what he was thinking.

"Don't say anything," she warned, hugging herself for warmth.

He merely shrugged as if it didn't concern him. "You really do make a good little savage," he said. "A few coincidences and you're ready to believe anything. Except reason. Or fact."

"That car was there," she answered. "That's a fact. And if I'd make a good savage, you'd make a terrible one. Your whole world is based on logic and law. How can you defend other people's spiritual beliefs when you don't want to have any yourself—beyond your precious reason?" She gave 'reason' the most ironic ring she could.

He threw her a lazy mocking glance, but didn't reply. He turned his attention back to the clouded road before them.

But the next time Piper looked at him, the expression on his face was odd, and if she hadn't known better, she would have thought it was troubled.

EVEN THOUGH IT HAD MEANT another flight over water, Piper was glad to be back in Kona, on the Big Island. For some reason she couldn't explain, she felt most at home there.

David took her to supper that evening at a small cozy restaurant down by the docks. She was surprised he bothered, for she hadn't been pleasant to him. His remarks about lust had hurt too deeply to let her smile and pretend everything was fine.

She was still disturbed, as well, over the news about MacDowell. Eloise had her son back at last and sounded happier than she had in years. Piper, however, barely remembered MacDowell, and unlike Eloise and Jeannie, she had no treasured memories of him. She had never felt any pangs of loss at his absence. To her mind, from childhood, it seemed perfectly right and natural that MacDowell was gone.

But she well knew that she had been raised to take his place, and she wondered now if she was any longer needed. He would take her place in the business, Eloise had hinted as much. Maybe he would even take her place in the family's affections. It was possible. What had she ever been, anyway, but his substitute?

She set down a french fry, barely touched. She wore a black skirt and matching cotton sweater and felt as drab as a crow, the only mournful thing in paradise.

David regarded her over his coffee cup, his frown line deepened. "What's the matter? Are you still upset about this morning?"

"No," Piper said and sipped her wine. "Why should I? It meant nothing."

He set down his cup. He wore a gray and muted blue Hawaiian shirt. "Look, Piper, it didn't exactly mean nothing. It means we feel a physical attraction for each other, that's all. It's normal."

She shrugged in response.

"And I have to admit," he said, frowning harder, "it's heightened by knowing we shouldn't do anything. Because of the ritual. The forbidden's always the most tempting."

"For the first time, I'm grateful for the stupid ritual," she said, and picked up the french fry again.

The corners of his mouth turned down. "You mean it's not really a match made in paradise—Eloise Claxton's granddaughter and a half-breed maverick lawyer."

She looked away. "I don't think of you as a half-breed. I think of you as a person."

He gave an ironic smile. "That's big of you."

"I didn't mean it that way."

He sighed harshly. "Look. All I'm saying is that what happened is natural. It's nothing to worry about."

"I'm not worried about it," Piper said and nibbled on the french fry.

"Then what *are* you worried about?" he demanded. "Because you look unhappy as hell."

She hesitated a moment, fiddling with an earring, then told him haltingly about Eloise being ill and that nobody had told her. Because he was a surprisingly good listener, she found herself telling him about MacDowell's return, about her family, Jeannie, Harold, the twins, everything.

"I don't believe this," he said when she finished. "You're just going to let them do this to you? For years she's groomed you for this job and now, suddenly, you have to give it up to the prodigal son?"

Piper instantly regretted confiding in him. "It's her business, they're her stores. She should do what she wants."

He gave a short humorless laugh. "I see," he said, but she could tell he didn't.

"She's had terrible responsibilities and worked hard all her life," Piper said, defending Eloise. "She should be able to use her wealth any way she likes."

"Piper, I understand the concept," he said, looking into her eyes. "But I don't agree with it. She can't play around with your future like you're a puppet on a string."

"I'm not a puppet," she returned with spirit.

He arched a cynical eyebrow. "No? You're here, aren't you? Doing what she wants even though you don't agree with it?"

"Yes? Well, you're here, too. Does that make you a puppet?"

"No. Whether or not I like your grandmother, I believe in native rights. At least I'm here because I believe in something. Not you. You're going against all your principles. You didn't want that necklace destroyed."

"I do believe in something," she said passionately. "I believe in my grandmother. I believe in my family. I'm glad MacDowell's coming back, for their sakes, but it seems...it seems they might not need me any longer."

"Piper, these people are adults. What right did they ever have to need you so much in the first place?" He shook his head in disgust. "Why, in the name of all that's holy, should it have ever been up to you to take care of everything? Why did you let yourself get in a position where she's got such control over your life?''

"That's not how it is," Piper protested. "I didn't mind trying to take care of everything. I love them. I'll love them if MacDowell is there or if he isn't. And there's nothing wrong with my grandmother's controlling what's hers.''

"Hers, hers, hers," he sneered. "In my family we didn't have much, but we shared. What was my grandfather's was *ours*. What was my aunt's was *ours*. What was Aaron's was *ours*. And what was mine was *ours*—including my trouble.''

"How noble," she said, angry at his criticism.

"Right, the noble savage," he said, nodding curtly for emphasis. "But let me tell you something. We gave what we could give willingly. Nobody bought anybody's affection or loyalty.''

"Can't you understand?" Piper argued. "She never bought anybody. She doesn't spoil Jeannie or Harold or me. She never promised me anything except responsibility, and MacDowell *isn't* coming home for her money. That's why they quarreled in the beginning, because she was giving most of the money to the museum. Why is that so different from your precious 'grave goods' that go to the dead? MacDowell couldn't accept it, but now apparently he can, and—''

He cut her off. "Let me tell you something," he said, leaning forward for emphasis. "I've been watching you, and I think I know your problem—''

"I don't have a problem. It's just a little hard to adjust—''

"Your problem is this—she's got you so brainwashed, you're frightened to death to be less than perfect. You're scared to death to show any weakness. You hate yourself for being human.''

"That's not true," Piper returned, anger burning her cheeks. "That's cheap amateur psychology."

"Is it? Well, here's more—you want to think you're fearless. That's how you seemed back in Nebraska where you're at home—absolutely fearless, confident. But once things started getting different, they started getting scary. And I don't think what scared you most was the ocean or the lizards. You were scared of being scared. You're terrified to find out you *can* feel fear."

"That's not true," she argued. "Every time I was scared, there was a good reason. I've always been the strong one. Always."

"So your grandmother's led you to think. But you don't feel right unless you're working and breaking your back to take care of things. You've been trained for nothing except duty, duty, duty. Without all those duties, without your family, you don't know quite who you are—and it scares the hell out of you. Being a woman scares the hell out of you."

In truth, he was not revealing anything Piper hadn't thought herself in the past few troubled hours, but she hated him for saying it. Perversely, she hated him for even understanding how she felt. "I'm not like that," she protested, her chest constricting with resentment.

"Not yet," he warned. "But all you've done your whole life is reflect *her,* her importance, her needs, her concerns—like a bright little mirror. But who are *you,* Piper? When there's no Eloise around to define you? No big responsibilities to give your orderly little life meaning?"

"Stop it," she said, glaring.

"No. And I'll tell you something. I hated living on the reservation. I hated it with all my heart. So I got out. I had to leave certain pieces of myself behind to do it, but I knew if I was ever going to find out who I was, who I could be, I had to leave."

"Maybe you left all your feelings behind," she said. "Can't you understand I love her? This is my *family*. These are my *people*."

"I'm trying to understand," he said. "But you know what the saddest thing is? She taught you everything about being strong. But nothing about being human. She never taught you it's all right for you to be afraid, for you to need somebody, for you to depend on somebody else. On a man, for instance."

"I don't need anybody," she answered angrily. "As for men, I never knew one I could depend on."

He stared at her, his face stony. "You've depended on me."

All her senses seemed to cartwheel in confusion. With shock she realized what he said was true. She had depended on him. Twice she had trusted her very life to him. He had even shed his blood to spare her pain.

"You think you have courage," he said. "Do you have the courage to defy her for once in your life?"

His look was so challenging that she found it hard to breathe evenly. "What are you talking about?"

"I'm talking about you and me. I know your grandmother hates me. That can't be helped. But I don't think you do. Not after this morning."

"This morning," she said unhappily, turning her face away. "Forget this morning."

"I think we should have an affair," he said bluntly.

Piper whirled to stare at him in astonished furor. *"What?"*

He nodded, his face as emotionless as if he had merely suggested they share a cab to the airport.

"We should have an affair. Nothing earthshaking, just get each other out of our systems. After the ritual's over, of course. I was planning to stay on here an extra week, anyway. Stay with me."

"Are you insane?" she asked, shaking her head in dazed wonder. "First you insult me. You tear me practically to shreds. Now you ask me to have an affair?"

"I find you attractive," he said, unsmiling. "Whether or not we like it, there's something between us. Physically, that is."

"I see," she said from between clenched teeth. "But not mentally, of course. Or emotionally."

"I like you well enough," he said, looking troubled again. "I'm even concerned about you. But I have to tell you up front you're not the type I'd settle down with. Not the sort I'd marry. I have to be honest about that."

She stared at him.

He shrugged, his expression growing harsh. "I told you. I always figured that if I ever get the urge to marry, I'd marry another Native American. You know, not dilute the blood any more. You'll marry one of your own kind, too. But that doesn't mean we can't be attracted to each other now. So stay with me. For a week. It could be...pleasant."

Piper refused to look at him any longer. She pushed back her chair and stood up. "This has been the worst day of my life," she said, grinding out the words.

He stood, too. "I asked you something."

She tossed him a brief fiery glance. "Do I want to have an affair with you? No. I'd rather have an affair with the devil. I'd rather have an affair with a ... bug."

She started past him, but he reached out, stopping her. "Because you're afraid of offending her? Your grandmother?"

"Oh, for heaven's sake," she said, trying to shake off his hand, "leave her out of this, will you? And let go of me."

David released her, but when Piper headed for the door, he threw several bills on the table and followed. He caught up with her just outside the restaurant. The night was balmy and the branches of a plumeria tree hung over the side-walk, dropping yellow petals on the breeze.

He seized her by the arm and halted her. "Don't run away from this," he ordered.

She tossed her head dangerously. "I'm not. I'm walking away. I intend to keep on walking. Why on God's green earth would I ever want to have an affair with *you?*"

When she tried to pull away, he drew her closer, his hands clamping over her upper arms. "Because you need it," he said, the line of his mouth almost cruel.

"I need it?" She gave a bitter laugh. "Don't flatter yourself."

He drew her closer still, bending over her in the dark-ness. "Then you *should* need it. If you've got a normal urge in your body. I think there are plenty in there, wanting out. Let them. Stay with me. A week. It just might do us both good."

She wanted to scream, strike his hands away from her, flee. Instead she stood, staring up at him fiercely, her heart thundering in her chest. "*Good* for us? You sound like you're suggesting we get flu shots together."

"All right," he said grimly, his hands tightening on her arms. "Maybe I haven't been romantic—"

"It doesn't matter how you ask it," Piper said angrily, "The answer is *no.*"

"But not because you're afraid?" he jeered.

"No," she retorted. "I'm not afraid." But she was lying. His suggestion had frightened her as much as it had in-censed her.

"No," he almost hissed, "you couldn't be afraid, could you? It's a sin for strong little Piper to be afraid."

She wrenched away from him and began walking toward the hotel. The night air was fragrant with flowers, and its warmth contrasted painfully with the coldness she felt settling around her heart. David stayed beside her, refusing to let her escape. "Are you listening to me?"

"Be quiet," she ordered. "I don't want to hear any more of this."

"You'll hear it anyway. It bothers you, doesn't it, being away from her and the rest of them? Have you really ever been away from them before?"

"Yes! I went away to college."

His mouth twisted skeptically. "I don't believe it."

"I did. For a semester. The University of Chicago."

"Then what happened?" he demanded.

"I went . . . home."

"Why?"

"Because. Because, that's all."

"So the independent career woman has only been away from Grandma twice in her life. Lord, Piper, when do you start to live for yourself? Did you even get to finish college?" He reached over, squeezing her arm for emphasis.

She jerked away from his touch, walking faster. "I came home because of my grandmother," she said furiously. "*You* nearly put her in the hospital. You dragged her into court and humiliated her, nearly ruined her name. No, I didn't finish. I had to straighten out the damage *you'd* done."

"I wasn't trying to inflict damage. If she'd kept decent records, there wouldn't have been any damage. I didn't take her to court for personal reasons. It was a simple native-rights case."

"But she wasn't guilty," Piper returned hotly. "You'll never make me believe she did it, never! Rights, rights, rights—you're always talking about rights. But you never talk about feelings."

She looked up at him, her face bitter. "I don't think you even understand the feelings people have about the neck-lace. All you understand is the part about *rights*. You understand legal things just fine, but emotional ones, no. You're a fine one to talk about *my* emotions."

She saw that somehow, blindly, she had struck home. His expression had taken on that impassive look he got when he didn't want his feelings to show.

"That's right, isn't it?" she taunted. "You can talk until you're blue in the face about respecting beliefs, but you'll never understand them. There's mystery all around us on these islands, but you'd never admit it. There's beauty and magic and color, but you don't want to see it. You want everything black and white, right and wrong, legal and illegal. Even an affair isn't a matter of feelings—it's something that'd be 'good' for us. Therapeutic. You wouldn't want any sloppy *feelings* mixed up in it. You're even going to pick out a bride by her bloodlines, as if she's a racehorse."

His face was more impassive than before. "That's different," he said.

"Yes. For you it's always different. You judge everybody. But nobody's supposed to judge you. Nobody's smart enough, are they?" she asked. "What's wrong with emotion, anyway? Do you think it's too primitive for you? Heaven knows, you don't want anybody thinking you're primitive, do you?"

For a long moment he gave her a look so cold that it frightened her, but she stared back, unflinching. "Well?" she said.

"Nothing," he said with a cool calm. "I'm sorry I suggested it. It would have been a little too Romeo and Juliet, wouldn't it? There's no peace between our houses. There never will be. And God knows, no love."

He glanced at his watch. "I'll take you back to the hotel. Then I've got to get going."

"Where?" she asked with sarcasm. "Going to look for your *woman* again?"

"As a matter of fact, yes."

She could no longer trust herself to speak. She was almost trembling with anger when he left her at the hotel.

She entered her room, and without bothering to turn on the light, she sat down on the edge of the bed and put her face in her hands. She wanted to weep, but she was too deeply wounded for tears.

He had said damning things about her and her family. What terrified her was that some of what he said had the ring of truth. Of what importance was her own life without the responsibilities Eloise had always placed in her hands? For Eloise, for Jeannie and Harold and even the twins, she had always tried to be fearless and strong. Always. But now they had found someone they thought to be even stronger. She was no longer needed.

The phone jangled in the darkness. Her heart began to beat wildly. Her grandmother—it could be no one else.

She fumbled for the receiver. "Yes?"

"Piper?" It was Eloise.

"Yes?"

"I've had so little chance to talk to you because of this business with the hospital and with MacDowell. I just wanted to know if you'd reached Kona safely."

"Yes," Piper said numbly. "We did."

"Your room is satisfactory, I take it?"

"Yes," she said, although all she could see around her was darkness.

"Good. Now I want you to call me tomorrow when all this ceremonial nonsense is over. I'll have a message for you to convey to Mr. Whitewater. All right?"

"All right," she said dully. A message, she thought, the words not really registering. For David?

"And Piper," Eloise said, "I don't want you worrying because MacDowell is back. There'll still be plenty for you to do. Once things are settled, I've been thinking of taking a long vacation. To Scotland. You could be my traveling companion. How would that be? A nice long vacation? Then we'll come back and see how you fit into Mac-Dowell's reorganization of the business. He thinks you should go back to college and finish. You wanted to go so badly once. You'd still like a degree in art history, wouldn't you?"

"Of course," Piper said as automatically as a robot, but her heart contracted unhappily. She had no desire to go to Scotland. She didn't want to be a mere traveling companion. And she didn't want MacDowell deciding her fate, no matter how competent and considerate he was. He had no right.

"Also, I've been thinking," Eloise went on. "I've certainly done my part by giving up the necklace. Losing the olivine still bothers me. Remember you promised to try to save some?"

"Yes?" Piper said, a lump forming in her throat.

"Be sure you try," Eloise said pleasantly. "Just one piece—as a souvenir. Even the volcano goddess couldn't begrudge me that. You'll do it, won't you?"

Piper sat, trying to think. The darkness seemed to pulse around her. "I—I—" she stuttered.

She wanted to say, *I can't*.

Instead, she managed once more to say, "Of course," because she could think of nothing else to say. After all, it was Eloise asking. How could she refuse to respect her grandmother's wishes? If she did, it would seem like an act of spite, the most sordid sort of jealousy over MacDowell's return home.

But, thought some traitorous part of her mind, what she was asking her to do was wrong. It was stealing. If Eloise would cheat now over the necklace, could she have cheated before? Was David right about the Navaho jewelry? The thought made her feel sick. It couldn't be true. Piper tried to push the idea away; she hardly heard the rest of what her grandmother said.

When Eloise hung up, Piper sat alone again in the darkness. At last she rose and opened the door to the tiny balcony. She couldn't see the ocean, but she could hear it, growling and purring like a restless beast.

If she raised her face, she could see the pure, clean of the stars. She looked at them a long time.

CHAPTER TEN

PIPER TRIED TO PUSH ASIDE her anxieties the next morning when she and David went to see the third woman about Pele. She no longer referred to the women as priestesses, and neither did David. Privately some dark fancy made her think of them as the Cloud Holders, sisters in spirit to the complicated goddess who had brought Piper to this island.

David had little to say, treating Piper with cool indifference. In turn, she was aloofly polite. An uncomfortable silence pressed around them as they drove to the city of Hilo.

Mrs. Hoike was old, rather deaf and nearly blind. She lived with her granddaughter in an apartment complex in Hilo. Bedfast, she nevertheless sat up straight, and she greeted David and Piper with smiles and nods. Her snow-white hair was freshly washed and waved. She wore a pink bed jacket and a fresh lei of yellow plumeria blossoms.

She seemed eager to talk. Piper and David sat in chairs on opposite sides of her bed.

"What you're doing," she said, shaking a gnarled finger at Piper, "it's right." Her voice was surprisingly strong, her English heavily accented.

"Yes?" Piper said. She wore a dusty rose dress with a full skirt and a high neck. The pearls her grandmother had loaned her were in her ears.

"It shows respect for the old ways," Mrs. Hoike said, and smiled.

Piper nodded, avoiding David's eyes. She could feel him watching her.

"Mrs. Hoike," David said. "What about the ritual it-self? We're told it's not actually Hawaiian."

The woman waved her hand, a brief impatient gesture. "That's not what matters. What matters is that you do it."

"Why?" Piper asked, puzzled. She still suspected the sorcerer of having made the whole ritual up, according to his own bizarre whim.

"The old ways," the woman said, nodding sagely, "were almost gone. People were taught to be ashamed of them. But that's not good. It's the past. It's what we were. How can we like who we are if we look down on our ancestors? Respect should be shown to them, and to their ways. What you're doing is correct."

"I see," said Piper.

"I am American," said the old woman, chuckling. "But I am Hawaiian, too. One of these things is not better than the other. Both are good. You show respect for the old ways, you show respect for me—for what makes me what I am. You understand?"

Piper nodded.

David cleared his throat. "Mrs. Hoike, the ritual says you're supposed to tell us about Pele. What would you like to say?"

She smiled, wreathing her face in wrinkles. "Say? I would like to say... nothing."

"Nothing?" Piper echoed.

"No." She shook her head, amused at her own change of mind. "No. I will say something. Here is what I'll say—*listen*."

Piper sat straighter in her chair. "Listen?"

Mrs. Hoike laughed. "Why should I tell you of Pele? The whole island is telling you about her. Listen to it. And to your heart."

"I—I don't understand," Piper said.

"Fire created this island," the woman said, twisting one of the pink ribbons on her bed jacket. "Pele at work is a terrible sight—and a wondrous one. She destroys—but she creates. I have seen stone turned to fire, running down the mountain destroying everything in its path. I have seen it dripping through the air from the cliffs, into the sea, where it steams. It cools and makes new earth. Fire. Air. Water. Earth. Things come, they go. They are transformed."

"Yes?" Piper said, fascinated. How old was the woman, she wondered. Eighty? Ninety? A hundred? How much had she seen? How many of the old secrets did she know?

There was a moment of silence. "And that," Mrs. Hoike said with a cryptic smile, "is all I have to say about Pele."

Piper wanted to ask the woman more, but she did not. She had the feeling Mrs. Hoike had seen David and her to satisfy her own curiosity, not theirs.

When they said goodbye, Mrs. Hoike clung to Piper's hand an extra moment. Then she reached up and patted Piper's cheek. "Do what is right," she said. "Listen to the island, to your own heart. And do what's right." Piper suddenly felt guilty, wondering if the woman somehow knew of Eloise's request to save one stone.

Outside, troubled, she spoke to David. "That woman had...something about her. She said almost nothing about Pele. But for the first time, when she talked, I almost believed."

David was silent. He opened the car door and helped her in. He got in on the driver's side.

"I mean, it's amazing." She stared, brooding, at the pale blooms of the orchid trees. "To think that all this beauty began in fire and violence. No wonder people believe Pele gets angry if you carry off what's hers."

"That's mostly a rumor spread by park rangers," David said grimly. He seemed deep in thought.

"What?" Piper asked, startled.

He put the car into gear. "Park rangers encourage the story. The area at the fire pit is a park. A thousand people a day come through. If everybody took home a chunk of lava, pretty soon there wouldn't be a park left."

"You mean you admit all this Pele business isn't true?"

He narrowed his eyes against the sunlight as he edged the car into the traffic. "I didn't say it wasn't true. I said a lot was rumor."

"Well, is it true or not?" she asked, perplexed.

"How do I know?" he asked, his brow wrinkling moodily. "People still take pieces of lava. Sometimes they send them back. Rangers say it happens all the time. A package arrives with a note saying to put the stuff back. Since they took it home, their taxes went up, their kids got rebellious, their cat got fleas, whatever. Happens all the time. You tell me if it's true."

"How can I tell you?" she asked. "How could I possibly know?"

He gave her a brief sideways look and said nothing.

She remembered Mrs. Hoike's words: "Listen. To the island. And your heart."

Piper listened. But the only sounds she heard from the island were sounds of traffic. And if her heart spoke, she was too unhappy to hear it.

ONCE MORE they made the strange journey up through the changing scenery of the mountain. Piper thought she was growing used to such swift and surreal transformations, but she was wrong.

Nothing could have prepared her for the eerie sights of Kilauea. David had warned her she would see craters at this volcano, not fire. The fire, Kilauea's most spectacular activity, could only be seen by helicopter. An ominous quiet hung over the park.

When Piper stepped from the car, she felt she was on a dark, alien and uneasy moon. The dormant crater on Maui, even cloaked in clouds and swept by cold, had a silent majesty, a peaceful dignity. But this place struck her as neither majestic nor peaceful. It was as vivid a picture of hell as she could imagine. A wasteland of black rubble stretched as far as she could see. The air was chilly, the sky clouded, and when the wind shifted it brought the stench of burning sulfur to her nostrils.

All around, steam rose from the cracked earth like a hoard of specters. In some places the lava lay in great cindery chunks. In others it had hardened into tortuous curves and ripples.

The landscape was a lifeless desert, but it stretched over live subterranean fires that sent their vapors snaking skyward. It seemed more underworld than mountaintop.

"Here," David said, leading her to a crack in the rubbled earth. A ragged cloud of steam pulsed out of the crack at irregular intervals, like the breathing of some hidden dragon. He took her hand and knelt by the hole. "Feel," he said, and held her hand near the steam.

She drew back from the sighing heat. "It's like magic," she said, taking another step away. "The breath of creation."

He stood, looking at her.

"But how can creation be so ugly?" she asked.

Steam rose, phantomlike, behind him. "They say beauty's in the eye of the beholder."

Beauty, she thought, in confusion and awe. There was a terrible beauty here, the beauty of fierce unadorned power. Such a place, she thought, inspired fear. Yet it didn't feel evil, only mysterious. At last she understood why people believed in Pele. The mountain was breathing. It felt *alive*.

"I've looked at a lot of landscapes lately," Piper said softly. "This one seems to be looking back."

He smiled his usual fleeting smile. "I'll take you to the fire pit. That's supposed to be where Pele lives."

The crater of the fire pit was huge, a great circular canyon. Tattered clouds of steam writhed from its depths. Piper couldn't see how deep it was, for a guardrail kept people back from the edge.

A few hardy tourists went out on a protected walkway for a better view. The wind blew and Piper pulled her sweater more tightly around her. This time she had taken David's word that it would be cold, and she had brought a heavy white cardigan.

Beyond the guardrail, near the crater's edge, lay a scattering of objects, a few spots of color in a stark landscape. At first Piper thought they were the litter of careless tourists. But looking more closely, she shivered. The items were offerings, she realized, gifts to Pele.

A pineapple sat there, a small heap of red berries, an orange, a few leis, and two half-empty gin bottles. There were also several small bundles tied up in leaves.

"Is that for Pele?" Piper asked, staring at them.

"Yes. People bring her gifts."

"Gin?" she said skeptically.

"She's said to be fond of gin. And a bite of pork. That's probably what's in those bundles."

She shook her head, then looked beyond the offerings to the twisting steam that rose out of the pit, vaporous and white.

"Here," he said, digging into the pocket of his jacket. "It's the olivine. And the leaf of a ti plant. They also say she likes a wrapping of ti leaves. If you're going to do this, you might as well do it right."

He dropped the ruined silver and the loose olivine stones into her hand. There were five, three of good size, and two smaller ones. In her hand he placed the ti leaf, long and dark green.

She stared at the gems. All Eloise wanted was one stone for a souvenir. Just one. She had willingly given up all the other jewels. To keep just one did not seem terribly wrong, Piper told herself. Not when David himself said that stories of Pele's jealousy were mostly rumor. No, she thought, Eloise was not wrong in wanting just one stone saved.

Still, Piper felt a twinge of guilt as she remembered that Mrs. Hoike had told her to do the right thing. She remembered the feel of the old woman's hand on her cheek. Mrs. Hoike had trusted her. But so did Eloise, and Eloise was her own blood.

"How do I do it?" she asked softly, still staring at the stones.

"Go under the guardrail. Don't set it with the other things. Somebody might take it. Wrap everything in the leaf, then throw it in the fire pit as hard as you can."

"But I'm not supposed to go past the guardrail," she said nervously. "That's why it's there."

"Other people have. You can do it. This time you're solo. You don't need my help."

She swallowed hard. She stepped under the railing and moved toward the pit. It frightened her already, yawning so vastly before her. She glanced around to see if a park ranger was watching, ready to arrest her. All she saw were a few scattered groups of tourists, more interested in snapping pictures than in noticing her. She neared the pit's edge, the black rubble crunching beneath her shoes.

Her back was to David, her shoulders squared. Slowly, with trembling hands, she arranged the silver and four olivine stones on the ti leaf. The fifth stone she awkwardly palmed in her left hand.

There, she thought, that wasn't so hard. No tongue of fire leapt up to rebuke her. No thunder shook the sky to accuse her of committing a wrong.

She twisted the leaf around the stones and took a step nearer the crater's edge. Briefly she glimpsed into the steaming depths of the pit. She squeezed her eyes shut, took a deep breath and hurled the stones as far as she could.

She did not hear them hit bottom. All she heard was the soft moan of the wind.

Quickly she turned, putting her left hand into the pocket of her sweater and dropping the stone into it. Everything was done. She and David were finished and at last she could go home. Yet she was sad and strangely empty, and the stone in her pocket made her feel treacherous, as well.

She slipped back under the guardrail and walked to David's side.

She looked at him. He wore a wine-colored sweatshirt, the hood down, and his dark hair tossed in the wind. He stared down at her, his face expressionless.

"Well," she said, "it's over."

He shifted his shoulders in a careless shrug. "Yes. It's over."

She tried to smile, but didn't succeed. "Now we can go home."

He shook his head. "You can. I told you. I'm staying a while. I want to see my brother. And I have . . . business to tend to. Somebody to see this afternoon."

Piper looked away, toward the clouds rising from the pit, white against the black stone. "Oh. Your woman friend? Did you find her last night?"

"More or less. But she—I have to see her again."

"I see." The lonesome wind moaned more forcefully. She wondered if the woman was Hawaiian, a Native American like himself. The sort of woman he really wanted.

He jammed his hands into the pockets of his jeans and, nodding for her to follow him, started toward the car. "So," he said, with the same restless shrug, "your plane doesn't leave till this afternoon. I'll drop you back at the hotel and go see her. Then I'll come back and take you to the airport."

"And that'll be it?" she asked with false brightness. "We'll say goodbye at last?"

He stared across the black wastes. "At last we'll say goodbye."

They drove most of the way back to Kona in silence. On the outskirts of town, she finally said, "Do you suppose we'll see each other again? Back in Nebraska?"

He smiled with a touch of bitterness. "We don't exactly travel in the same circles. Your family considers me an enemy, remember? You should remember. You've told me often enough. You'll go your way. I'll go mine."

A hollow sickness settled in her stomach. "Right." It was all she could think of to say.

He pulled into the hotel parking lot. "I'd walk you to your door, but I'm running a little late. I'll see you in a couple of hours."

He got out, the perfect gentleman, and opened her door. He stood for a moment, looking down at her. "See you," he said.

She nodded, a lump in her throat. He got back into the car and drove off.

She looked after him a moment. She tried to swallow the lump that choked her, but couldn't.

She walked slowly to her room. It was the same one she'd had the first time in Kona, with its view of the parking lot.

She took off her sweater and took the olivine from the pocket. She set the gem beside the phone, and its green sparkled dully in the sunlight that poured through the window. She remembered the sunlight of that other clean-washed morning when she and David had almost made love.

She sat on the bed and dialed her grandmother. The phone rang several times before her grandmother's clipped voice answered, "Hello?"

"It's Piper," she said, wishing her voice didn't sound so spiritless. She paused. "It's over. It's done."

She heard a long exhalation of satisfaction from the other end. "Ah. Good. It's cost me a fortune, but at least I have those pesky native-rights people out of my life—for the time being."

Yes, thought Piper, they're out of our life. David would go on fighting for justice for his people, and she would go on—doing what?

"Did you save the olivine?" Eloise asked.

Piper felt the sickness knotting in her stomach more powerfully than before. "Yes."

"Good. And you should be home by tomorrow. You won't have to suffer that Whitewater creature any longer."

"No," Piper said. "I won't." She put her hand on her stomach, wondering if she were getting an ulcer.

"I'm going to have that olivine made into a ring for you," Eloise said. "As a reward for putting up with that beast. It will be my gift to you. You always loved that necklace. Well, he got what he wanted. It's destroyed. I hope he's happy."

Piper said nothing. She was too burdened with conflicting emotions.

"That man maddens me," Eloise said. "Thank heaven I didn't have to travel with him. I'd have torn him to shreds. I could hardly stand the thought of your being with him. I don't trust him for a minute, but thank heaven I can trust you."

Piper flinched, experiencing twin surges of unhappiness and guilt.

"I'll be glad to have you home," Eloise said. "Mac-Dowell wants you to help find him a house. And I need you to keep Jeannie in line. She's been very rambunctious since MacDowell's come home. She will *not* listen to me. Now she's got it into her head that she wants to go to work—in a library. A library! And MacDowell's encouraging her. Imagine! MacDowell also thinks that Harold should have more responsibilities, which, of course is ridiculous. You're going to have to help me convince him he's wrong.''

Piper felt a sudden wave of rebelliousness. ''MacDowell's right,'' she said shortly. ''Listen to him.''

There was a moment of ominous silence. At last Eloise spoke. ''What?''

''Listen to MacDowell. I won't help you take a stand against him. You wanted him home. If you want him to stay home, you should listen to him.''

''Piper,'' Eloise said, ''I don't believe this. You hardly know MacDowell. You're siding with him against me? What is this? Some kind of punishment because your feelings are hurt? I've always tried to do everything for you. The least you can do is—''

''The least I can do is tell you the truth,'' Piper said, her patience exhausted. ''You can't depend on me to keep the peace for everybody. You have to learn to deal with them yourself—all of them. Jeannie and MacDowell and Harold, too.''

Eloise's voice assumed a familiar haughtiness. ''Now who are you, miss, to tell me what I need to learn? I've taught you everything you know—''

''But there are things I still don't know,'' Piper said with feeling. ''There are things I still have to find out about myself and my future. Maybe it's time I did.''

''Oh, good heavens,'' Eloise said with profound disgust. ''You sound just like MacDowell did twenty years ago. The search for your identity, the freedom to be yourself. Oh, Lord, such rot. Well, MacDowell went running off looking for himself, and where did he end up? Right back home, that's where. Which is where you belong, too.''

''At least MacDowell went out and looked. At least he'd seen the world when he made the decision to come home.''

"Piper," Eloise admonished, "what are you saying? That you want to leave home? Nonsense! Come back right now. I've already told you. I'm willing to send you back to college. We'll talk about it tomorrow."

Thoughts spun through Piper's head so swiftly they dizzied her. At the same time she seemed to be thinking with amazing clarity. "I won't be home tomorrow," she said firmly. "I have to stay here one more day."

"Stay?" exploded Eloise. "Another day? Do you know how expensive it is? Do you know I'll have to pay a penalty if you change your plane ticket this late? A hefty one? I just offered to sent you back to college. I think that's quite enough generosity on my part."

"I'll pay my extra expenses, the plane fare, too," Piper said. "I have money in the bank. And if I decide to go back to college, I can put myself through. I'm not afraid of work. I don't want any gifts." Her own words surprised her, but she knew they were right. It was time for her to try to succeed on her own, without Eloise's help. It was time at last for her to go her own way.

"You're jealous that MacDowell's come home," Eloise accused. "That's not fair. He's my only son. I have a right to have him home, Piper. And I'm trying to make up to you for anything you might feel you've lost because he's come back. I'm taking you to Scotland. I'm sincerely trying to be as generous as possible."

"I don't want to go to Scotland," Piper said with fervid conviction. "Anything I've done for you, I've done for love. I didn't do it for rewards. I'm not jealous of MacDowell. I'm happy for you. But he's there now to take care of things. I'll have to find my own way. It's my turn now."

"Piper," Eloise said, her voice trembling with accusation, "it's not that Whitewater man, is it? Has he turned you against me? He dragged our good name through the mud. He persecuted me—I didn't know that Navaho jewelry was false—I've never done anything dishonest in my life. You must believe that—never. You do, don't you?"

"Yes. I believe you," Piper said, tears stinging her eyes. She wanted to believe her grandmother, but Eloise had asked her to keep the olivine. Wasn't that dishonest? Wasn't it wrong?

As for David, what did it matter if she cared for him, when he didn't care for her? Other than his cavalier suggestion of a week-long affair, he had offered her nothing. He had no use for her.

"You cannot become involved with that man," Eloise stated flatly. "He's not our kind. Oh, he's a fine foe. I'll give him that. A woman couldn't ask for a worthier enemy. But I'll show him. MacDowell's taking that case back to court. This time I'll have *Mr.* Whitewater and his precious organization ground into the dust. *He'll* see."

"What?" Piper asked, alarmed.

"I'm innocent," Eloise said. "And MacDowell's willing to fight to prove it. We're going to appeal the case. This time we'll beat Whitewater, and his pride can be broken for a change. Tell him *that.* I intend to appeal and to win. MacDowell says I shouldn't care if it takes a fortune. He wants the dirt cleaned off the family name. And so, at long last, do I."

War, Piper thought sickly. War again between David and her grandmother. Between her people and his. Her loyalties and his.

"Furthermore," Eloise went on coldly, "MacDowell thinks we should have fought for the necklace. Maybe we still will. He's checking it out with lawyers right now."

"No!" Piper retorted with another surge of rebellion. "You can't! It's wrong! The necklace was never yours to begin with. It belonged to the Hawaiian people. It belonged to the chief. Fighting would be wrong. I won't hear of it. I won't come home at all if you do that. I mean it."

"Piper, are you defying me? It *is* that man, isn't it? Are you siding with him against your family? Do you remember what he did to me?"

"If you want to reopen the case about the Navaho jewelry, that's your business," Piper said, shaking her head. "Do what you have to. But you said the necklace wasn't worth fighting for. Don't change your mind after all I did. I mean it. And please don't be so vindictive. That's wrong, too. And it's not good for you."

"Oh, Piper," Eloise said impatiently, "stop lecturing me. We'll discuss it later. I don't intend to do anything unreasonable. Just come home. Now. We've got a trip to Scotland to plan."

"I can't come home yet," Piper said. "I have to stay a little longer."

Eloise gave a snort of barely disguised disgust. "Get packed and get on the plane immediately. That's an order. You have no further business in Hawaii."

"I do," Piper said, her voice as stubborn as Eloise's. "I have to stay. I finally heard what this island has to say."

"Piper, have you gone mad? Islands don't talk. Whatever's happened to you?"

Piper picked up the olivine and fingered it. "Hawaii happened to me," she said. "And I have to let it keep happening. For just one more day. I have things I'm still learning."

"Madness," Eloise said contemptuously, but she sounded hurt, as well.

"I love you," Piper said. "But I have to find out who I am without you."

"Piper, if you're involved with that Whitewater man, I could never forgive you. I just don't think I could. Have you no family pride? What *is* going on in your head? That man almost ruined me. Oh, I know he'll say he was only doing his job, but—"

"I can't talk about it anymore," Piper answered, tears burning her eyes. "We'll talk when I get home."

"Come home now."

"I can't," said Piper.

Eloise hung up on her. When Piper heard the receiver slam down, she felt as if part of herself had been severed. Never before had she disagreed so bitterly with her grandmother. Never before had the words they exchanged been so harsh, so divisive. She put her hands to her face, and clutching the olivine, she wept.

CHAPTER ELEVEN

DRY-EYED AT LAST, Piper felt numb but restless, almost dangerously full of energy. She had to have physical activity, she thought, or she would explode.

The hotel had a saltwater lagoon, a natural pool of calm water separated from the sea by a chain-link fence. Almost mechanically, she put on her bathing suit and went to swim. She swam back and forth, ignoring the sting of the salt until she was exhausted and her back sunburned.

When she could swim no longer, she put on her beach coat and aimlessly explored the hotel grounds. She saw a lizard basking on a stone wall. She forced herself to approach it and try to catch it.

At first her reluctant hands were too slow, but the animal was sluggish with the sun and did not move quickly. Tensing her body, she made herself keep trying. On the sixth attempt she caught it.

Shaking, she held it. It was small, perhaps six inches long, and green. It's little body was warm and, just as David had said, soft as velvet. She could feel its tiny heart beating against her hand, and knew it was far more frightened than she was. Every detail of it was as perfect as a jewel from Eloise's finest store, from its finely cut nostrils to the curling tip of its tail.

Carefully, she set it free, then stood staring after it as it scuttled away.

"What was that about?" a familiar slightly raspy voice asked from behind her. She whirled.

David stood in the shade of a plumeria tree. The grass around him was scattered with its yellow blossoms.

He took a step toward her, looking intently at her wet suit, her damp hair, her lips free of makeup. "Have you been swimming? In the *ocean?*"

She nodded, her heart beating faster than when she had held the lizard. "In the lagoon."

He gave a crooked smile of disbelief. "It's wet. It's salty. It's got fish in it."

"The fish and I learned to coexist."

"Did you just catch a lizard?"

"Yes." She tried to take a deep breath, but couldn't. She could barely take a shallow one.

The frown line appeared between his eyes. "Why? Why the water? Why the lizard?"

"Because I was scared of them."

He frowned and half smiled at the same time. "Are you still scared?"

She stood a bit straighter. "Not as much."

"Well," he said, his eyes on her. "Well, well, well."

They studied each other almost like adversaries.

"I want you to take me back to the volcano," she said.

His smile faded. "You've got a plane to catch."

"No. I canceled my flight. I've got to go back to the volcano. There's something I didn't do. Will you take me, or do I hire a cab?"

She knew what she had to do. She hoped that someday Eloise would understand, too.

"Piper," he said, taking another step toward her, "what is this? Listen, we've got to talk. I've found out something—"

"No," she said, holding up her hand to silence him. "I have things to tell you, too. But I don't want to talk until we get there. I won't talk about it. We have to go to the volcano first."

He seemed about to put his hands on her arms, then checked himself. The muscle in his cheek ticked, just once. "All right," he said at last. "Change your clothes."

He looked almost as troubled as she felt. Something in his eyes hurt and worried her.

Please don't hate me for what I have to tell you, she thought, biting her lip. Then she looked away, unable to meet his disturbing gaze any longer.

FIFTEEN MINUTES LATER they were in his car, headed once more for the heights of Kilauea. Piper wore the dusty-rose dress again, and although she'd showered and washed her hair, she hadn't bothered to dry it. She sat, leaning her aching head against the side window, trying to think of how she would confess to David about the olivine.

She would have to tell him, as well, that her grandmother intended to fight him in court again, this time with MacDowell's determined help. If David had a shred of liking or respect for her or her family, it would soon vanish. Eloise was determined to see to that.

"Isn't there a fern forest up by the crater?" she asked, her head still pressed against the glass.

"Yes. Why?"

"Because I'd like to go there afterward. Someplace quiet. Where we can talk."

His lips thinned in frustration. "Piper, I don't know what this is about, but I have to tell you something—"

"No." Stubbornly she shook her head, and unshed tears trembled in her eyes. "Not now. After the volcano."

He exhaled harshly, started to speak again, then stopped. They drove on in silence.

How can I tell you what I've done? she wondered miserably. Then to fill the silence, which throbbed awkwardly about them, she asked, "Did you finish your book? *Gone with the Wind?*"

"Yes," he said, his voice clipped. "Last night."

She ran her fingers over her damp hair. "And? Did you like it?"

"No," he answered as he turned the car into the parking lot. "Scarlet was stupid. She let Rhett get away. She never understood that he loved her. Or that she could hurt him."

There was another moment of silence. "How could she understand he loved her?" Piper said. "He never told her." She closed her eyes against the ache in her head.

"Why did he have to tell her? She should have known," he said. "How could she not have known?"

As soon as he parked the car, she put on her sweater, got out and strode purposefully toward the fire pit. This time the black-and-white starkness of the scene didn't seem as foreign to her. Her emotions felt at home in these desolate wastes.

David caught up with her and tried to take her arm. She eluded him and hurried on. "Piper," he said, frustration roughening his voice.

She ducked under the guardrail and marched toward the crater's edge, the wind eddying her full skirt around her legs.

"Piper," he repeated, "be careful. Don't get so close." He followed her under the railing and once again caught up with her at the fire pit's edge. "Be careful . . . What are you doing?"

She reached into her pocket, her fingers curling around the olivine. She drew it out, clenched in her fist. She opened her hand and showed him.

"I kept one," she said, her chin trembling in grief and anger at what she had done. "My grandmother asked me to, and I did. It was wrong."

"Piper," he said, a strange look lighting his eyes, "don't. If she . . ."

But Piper didn't listen. She drew back her arm and threw the stone as hard as she could into the fire pit. Wisps of steam rose up from its depths—ghosts finding their way to heaven.

"Now," she said, turning to face him. "Let's go somewhere and talk."

As she stared up at him, her heart beat harder than it had in the thin air of the House of the Sun. She noticed, dazedly, that the expression on his handsome face was slightly stunned.

"This may be some talk," he said, and shook his head.

THE FERN FOREST did not seem real, which suited Piper's mood perfectly. Not far from the barren moonscape of the volcano, an improbably lush rain forest flourished, nurtured by cloud covers and the rain-bearing trade winds. The ferns grew as tall as trees, like something from a prehistoric tableau.

"Another of the thousand faces," she said, looking up at the ferns in wonder. They were giant, yet delicate, like plants in a dream or a fairy tale.

This island isn't possible, she thought. This island isn't real. Things are always changing into other things. Pele or no Pele, this island is magic.

She and David stood at the edge of a path that led into the forest's green heart. He reached over and took her hand, which surprised her. His touch sent fine tremors coursing through her.

"You have things to say to me," he said, "and I have things to say to you. Who goes first?"

"You can," she said, She didn't know how to explain keeping the olivine. And she didn't know what he would say when he learned her grandmother was ready for another court battle. She savored the feel of her hand in his and wondered if it might be the last time they'd touch so.

"All right," he said. "I think we'd better sit down. I have two things to tell you."

He stopped by a fallen tree. "Sit," he said, his hand still around hers. She sat, and he settled beside her, his wide shoulder brushing her slender one.

He was silent a moment. "I met a woman last night," he said, his face impassive. "Her name is Maureen Mc-Murphy Shimodo. She's a pearl dealer."

"I've heard of her," Piper said, surprised. "That's the woman my grandmother got the necklace from."

"Yes." David squeezed her hand, then set his jaw and spoke stiffly. "Maureen Shimodo once sent your grandmother a shipment of low-grade cultured pearls that were supposed to be natural pearls. She claimed she didn't know it herself—a cut-rate wholesaler had bilked her. At any rate, she ended up owing your grandmother a lot of money—which she didn't have."

"I know," Piper said, wondering why he was telling her all this. It was ancient history. "Instead of taking her to court, Grandmother took the necklace instead."

He took a deep breath. "Piper," he said carefully, "when I was reading up on all this back in Nebraska, right before we left, I reviewed some old records in which Maureen Shimodo claimed to have been cheated. I'd never seen the information before, but it rang a bell. The whole affair sounded too much like what your grandmother claimed happened to her with the Navaho jewelry."

He frowned, staring down at their linked hands. "There were differences between the two stories, but important similarities. A large dark man makes each woman an offer too good to refuse. He also offers a fat bonus if they pay cash. Both women should know better, but neither can resist. He writes them receipts, but they're worthless, just scrawls with a phony name and false address."

He shook his head. "In Maureen Shimodo's case, he says he's Tahitian. In your grandmother's he says he's a Navaho. Yet the two cases happened twenty years apart. Was it coincidence? Or had your grandmother needed an alibi and simply stolen Maureen Shimodo's story and changed it?''

He frowned harder, squeezing Piper's hand so hard it almost hurt. ''But why would she use an alibi nobody had bought before? Was she desperate? Foolish? What? It nagged at me.''

He grimaced. ''Piper, when I prosecuted your grandmother I truly believed she was guilty. She had hardly any proof in her defense. And she was the most arrogant damned woman I ever met. I was . . . younger, and arrogant myself. She and I took one look at each other and wanted to beat the other one so badly we could both taste it. Neither one of us could stand losing.''

He drew a deep breath, his thumb playing over her knuckles. ''I decided when we came here to try to find Maureen Shimodo and check things out. What I hoped was that she could tell me something that would convince me I'd always been right—that your grandmother was guilty. Any resemblance between what happened to her and Maureen Shimodo was either a coincidence or a lie snatched up in desperation.''

Pausing, he looked down into her eyes and the muscle at the corner of his mouth twitched. ''Piper, the better I came to know you, the more this thing bothered me. At first I wanted to prove she was guilty so you'd believe me, trust me, not her. But I finally understood how much you loved her. You and I saw two different Eloise Claxtons. I wanted you to understand other people's ways. But I wouldn't understand your family's ways. Do you see?''

Piper swallowed and nodded.

''I was pushed in opposite directions,'' he said, staring at their locked hands again. ''I wanted to be right. I wanted to be wrong. At first I wanted her to be guilty for my sake.

Then I wanted her to be innocent for your sake. And she *is* innocent. Maureen Shimodo can prove it.''

Piper blinked hard. He was a proud man and she knew how much this admission was costing him, but she was confused. ''But, David,'' she said, shaking her head, ''you made me wonder if—almost made me suspect that—maybe she was guilty.''

''Dammit, Piper,'' he said, taking her other hand in his, ''don't you see? All the evidence was against her. Nobody had this other information at the time. We fought hard, and I won. No wonder she hates me.''

''But...'' Piper said, relieved and perplexed at once, ''now you have proof? That can clear her?''

''They caught the man in Australia two years ago. He died before he could be brought to trial,'' David said.

Piper could see how painful it was for him to admit he had been wrong, but she loved him for his integrity.

''He'd worked three continents for almost thirty years. His base of operations was Hong Kong. There were similar cases against him down under. Maureen Shimodo has a lot of connections with jewelry dealers in the Pacific. She heard through the grapevine about his arrest and checked him out. It was the man who'd cheated her, all right. And she's sure he's the one who cheated your grandmother. She said she'd known it all along.''

Piper stared up into his face, which was more solemn and troubled than before. ''But if she knew, why didn't she say something? Why didn't she come forward?''

He shook his head again. ''Piper, your grandmother drives a hard bargain. She forced Maureen Shimodo to give up the necklace or be prosecuted. If your grandmother suffered, what did Maureen care? Maureen hated her. It was sweet revenge. Eloise had fallen into exactly the same trap. Maureen Shimodo wouldn't have told *me* if I hadn't acted as if I were about to haul her into court for withholding evidence. If your grandmother thinks I was tough with her, she should have seen me pry the truth out of Maureen Shimodo. It took some doing. The woman's hard as nails."

"And now that you have the truth?" Piper said, watching how deeply the frown line etched itself between his brows.

"I'll tell her," he said, still holding both her hands and squeezing them hard. "She should go back to court and clear her name."

"What?" Piper breathed. "Oh, David," she said, shaking her head. "She is. She already plans to. She swears this time she'll beat you. She told me this afternoon. She'll put up a terrible fight, too, now that MacDowell's behind her. He's as stubborn as she is. It'll be terrible."

"No, it won't," he said, framing her face with his hands and smoothing back her hair. "Listen, Piper, there won't be any fight. The conviction was unjust, and it'll be overturned. When I took your grandmother to court, I never wanted to hurt her or her family. I only wanted justice. It's all I want now. I'll gladly apologize to her, even if she won't accept it. Maybe we've all been too blindly loyal to our own sides, to our own people to have been fair in this whole thing. But I'm tired of the bad blood between us. I'm on her side this time. I'm on your side."

Tears sprang once more into Piper's eyes, and one spilled over, running hotly down her cheek. David wiped it away with his thumb.

"I never believed she'd commit a fraud," Piper said, shaking her head. "I know she has flaws, but I didn't think she'd be dishonest. I had to believe she was innocent. But then, when I started thinking about the olivine, I started to worry and wonder..."

"Don't worry and wonder anymore," he assured her. "It's going to be all right. You've got to believe that."

"Oh, David," Piper said, and leaned her forehead against his shoulder. She felt almost free, almost secure, but still she was worried. "She was ready to fight you all over again. I hated it. I was sick. Sick. I didn't want her hating you—and wanting me to hate you, as well. Not you. She wants to fight you over the necklace, too. I tried to stop her, but I don't know if I can."

"She won't want to fight for long," he said, his arm around her. "Piper, don't worry. The necklace is a different matter. Any sane judge would throw the case out of court. She doesn't like to waste money. She's just got her dander up now. She'll see the light."

"She has to," Piper said, her face pressed against the warmth of his chest. "She can't go on being bitter. It isn't good for her. It isn't good for...any of us." Her voice broke and she felt her tears wetting his shirt. "I'm sorry I tried to steal the olivine. I wanted to prove to her that I loved her, no matter what. I hated myself, David."

"It's all right," he said, stroking her hair. He paused, seeming to search for words. "Piper, don't cry. I know she won't like what you did, and for a moment there, I almost didn't want you to defy her, to hurt your relationship with her. I didn't want you to do anything that would make you unhappy. But it's done. You've got to believe this—you knew the right thing and you did it. Don't cry—it'll make me crazy. I can't stand it. Listen. I have one more thing to tell you. Listen to me. Please."

She rested against his shoulder, waiting. A sense of ease began to warm her, making her feel that things might somehow work out, after all.

"I don't know how to say this," he said.

He drew her upright so that he could look into her face.

She stared at him questioningly, blinking back her tears of relief. His jewel-blue eyes were more troubled than before. "Can you stand to hear more?" he asked, touching his forefinger beneath her chin.

She nodded, waiting.

He took a deep breath. He put his hands on her shoulders, gripping them tightly. "After I talked to Maureen Shimodo I went and sat by the sea. Just sat and thought. I thought about you. And about your grandmother. She may always see me as the enemy."

Piper nodded, not quite comprehending. She knew Eloise was not a forgiving soul, except perhaps to her own flesh and blood.

"She may hate me until the day she dies," David said solemnly. "And I have no right to ask you to choose between her and me. No right."

Piper bit her lower lip softly, never taking her eyes from his face.

"I guess," David muttered, searching her face, "what I'm trying to say is that I don't want to make the same mistake Rhett Butler did. I don't want to be too proud to say I love you. If you turn from me, knowing that, it's one thing. But if I never told you, and I lost you because of that, then..."

He didn't finish the sentence. For once in his life he couldn't seem to find words easily. He shook his head. Then he bent and kissed her. "I want you," he said against her lips. "And I love you."

She felt an odd jarring sensation, as if the world had suddenly stopped spinning. He drew back and his face hovered over hers, inches away. She looked up at him in disbelief. "You... love me?" she asked hesitantly.

His hands tightened once more on her shoulders. His mouth moved with an intensity of feeling. "I want you. You should have known from the first. Only then, I just wanted the physical part of you. Now I want all of you. Yes. I love you."

Her breathing became tight again, her head felt giddy, but an unexpected happiness tingled through her veins. "You and me?"

"Yes," he said. "You and me." He took her face between his hands. "At first I thought you were the most perfect little thing I'd ever seen. Skin like silk, hair like silk, every movement like silk."

Her pulses beat beneath the heat of his fingers as his face drew nearer to hers.

"At first I didn't understand you," he said, frowning. "At first you seemed cold and fearless. But you weren't. You were warm and human. And even when you were afraid, you kept going."

For the first time Piper realized, dazedly, that she understood what was at the heart of what she feared during this strange trip. She had feared change. The moment she had seen David Whitewater, her mind, her heart, her world began to change, to transform, and she had been fearful of what it meant.

"For years, I've been a fighter," he said, staring down into her face, his thumb stroking her cheek. "I fought, but in an important way, I forgot what was at stake. I only understood I had to fight for my people."

He tipped her face closer to his, brought his own nearer. "But I didn't want to see the world in the old ways of my people, the mysterious ways. Aaron always did, but not me. I was too busy being the way you said—all logic, all black and white, not wanting to show emotion. I knew feelings hurt, and I'd used the white man's weapons—logic, technology, law—as long as I didn't want to admit I had feelings left. I tried to kill them."

His mouth became a taut line as he stared into her eyes. "But you. You were full of feeling. Every time you looked around this place, you saw beauty and danger and secrets lying beneath the surface. Everything you looked at, you saw in the old way—in wonder—as it should be seen. As I should have been seeing it all along."

He kissed her again.

Stunned, Piper found herself kissing him back almost reverently, as if they were doing something wonderful and fearful when they touched.

He drew back from her again, his face tense with hope. "Does that mean you love me, too?"

Unable to speak, she nodded.

"Then stay with me," he said, his face more intent than before. "Stay with me for good. Marry me."

"But I'm not your kind," she said. "You told me that. More than once."

"I told myself that, too. I kept telling it to myself. It was a lie. You're my kind. You're the heart of my heart. I began to suspect it on the green sand beach. But I fought admitting it. Do you know when I knew for sure?"

She shook her head, and once again tears threatened to blur her vision.

"When I tried to say goodbye to you earlier," he said, his face solemn. "And I felt how much it hurt. It hurt as if something had died in me."

She smiled in happiness, her lips trembling.

"If you're going to marry me, kiss me," he said.

She parted her lips and let him take them. His arms wound around her so tightly she could barely breathe, but she didn't mind; she wished he would hold her even tighter. She wrapped her arms around the solid column of his waist and reveled in the deepness of his kiss.

David pulled away from her slightly, but his mouth still almost touched hers. "Do you understand what this means? What it might do to your relationship with your grandmother?"

She remembered Eloise's words: "If you're involved with that Whitewater man, I could never forgive you. I just don't think I could." Eloise would be pulled in two directions, as Piper had been ever since she'd met David.

But she loves me. She does, and she'll forgive me, even though it's going to be difficult, Piper thought. She has to, I know she will, no matter how long it takes.

Eloise would some day understand and forgive Piper, just as she had forgiven MacDowell. Eloise could never really shut out her own. Any more than Piper could bar Eloise from her heart. It was impossible. And David would give Eloise one of the things she wanted most in the world: proof of her innocence. Yes, Eloise would accept him. Piper knew it. "I love you," she said. The corners of her mouth turned up and she gave a small shaky laugh. "So Eloise will have to learn to like you. And you'll have to learn to like her—no matter what it takes out of the both of you."

"She's probably going to want to disown you at first," he said, concern in his eyes. "If you want a career, you'll probably have to start over again from the bottom."

"I've been thinking of going back to college, anyway," she told him. "People start over all the time."

He looked at her for a long moment. "Yes," he said. "They do."

He kissed her again. Then he rose and drew her to her feet. "Let's go back to the hotel," he said. "I'll call Aaron and tell him I'm going to be a couple of days late. I'm not sharing you with anybody else yet. Not after all we've been through. I want to get married before we go back to Nebraska. And I want to bring you back here every year. Here, to the place I really found you."

She nodded, her knees feeling slightly weak. She lay her face against his shoulder. "It's been a strange journey, hasn't it?"

"Hey," he said, drawing her close and kissing the top of her head. "It's just the start. This one lasts a lifetime."

She nodded, feeling the strong beat of his heart against her cheek.

He kissed her forehead, then her lips. Piper said nothing, only leaned against the secure hardness of his chest.

A journey that lasts a lifetime, she thought, suddenly almost frightened. The future stretched before her, a strange and unknown territory. Eloise would not map it for her or be able to guide her through it. She would have to find her own way, she . . . and David.

He hugged her. "I think I want to buy a marriage license before the sun goes down. The ritual's finally over and I have some very unchaste thoughts on my mind."

He stepped back from her and toward the path. He stopped and stared at her. Slowly he smiled his half smile.

She stood, looking at him, still disquieted by the newness of everything, by the new life she was choosing.

She held her breath and listened to the sounds of the forest and to the pulse of her uneasy heart.

Go, they seemed to say. *Go with him.*

"Are you ready?" he asked, and reached out his hand to her.

Go with him, said the breeze.

I love you, she thought, staring up into his eyes. *I'll always love you.*

She put her hand in his and went.

A LITTLE GIRL in red shorts and a red-flowered shirt came running down the path from the fern forest behind them. She was a beautiful half-caste child with the tawny skin and coppery hair sometimes seen on the islands.

She wore white plastic sunglasses ornamented with red plastic bows, and in her arms she carried a plush toy dog. The dog was white.

She stopped short when she saw David and Piper walking away from the forest. She stood staring after them, her face perfectly expressionless. She watched as David leaned over and kissed Piper on the ear, and Piper smiled up at him.

The child hugged the toy dog more tightly. She watched after them a moment longer.

Then she turned and ran lightly back up the path, vanishing in the shadows of the great ferns.

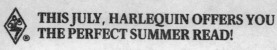

THIS JULY, HARLEQUIN OFFERS YOU THE PERFECT SUMMER READ!

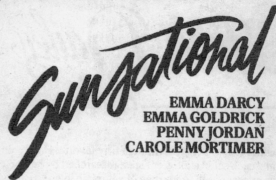

**EMMA DARCY
EMMA GOLDRICK
PENNY JORDAN
CAROLE MORTIMER**

From top authors of Harlequin Presents comes
HARLEQUIN SUNSATIONAL, a four-stories-in-one
book with 768 pages of romantic reading.

Written by such prolific Harlequin authors as Emma Darcy,
Emma Goldrick, Penny Jordan and Carole Mortimer,
HARLEQUIN SUNSATIONAL is the perfect summer
companion to take along to the beach, cottage, on your
dream destination or just for reading at home in the warm
sunshine!

Don't miss this unique reading opportunity.

Available wherever Harlequin books are sold.

SUN

Back by Popular Demand

Janet Dailey
Americana

A romantic tour of America through fifty favorite Harlequin Presents, each set in a different state researched by Janet and her husband, Bill. A journey of a lifetime in one cherished collection.

In August, don't miss the exciting states featured in:

Title #13 — ILLINOIS
The Lyon's Share

#14 — INDIANA
The Indy Man

Available wherever
Harlequin books are sold.